To Diana and Ian
with lots of love

The town of Sedgemouth, Bliss's store, and all the people in this book are entirely imaginary.

I

Bertram Archibald Bliss sat at his office desk, fingers lightly linked across a sheet of virgin blotting-paper, brooding about the female pulchritude that throbbed throughout the store below.

His mother, in her younger days a piano teacher, had chosen his names. Blinded by *folie de grandeur,* she had failed to realise the significance of the initials: her son, until he learned the art of concealment, suffered the burden of his obvious nickname and was mocked for years by cries of 'Baby', 'Babs' and 'Girly'. Nature and heredity combined to aid his tormentors: he never grew tall; he had fine, fair silky hair and a pale complexion, often pimpled. His eyes, the colour of aquamarine, were set under sparse blond brows; a nondescript nose and small button mouth completed his unremarkable features. Had it not been for his unusual names, he might have been an insignificant person all his life. As it was, a spark of rebellion was fired within him at an early age by the gibes of his schoolfellows; it was fanned by a desire to prove to his mother, who was widowed when he was five, that her faith in naming him extravagantly was justified. He never blamed her for the teasing he was forced to endure; spurred on by her belief in him, he determined to make his mark upon the world. He would show all who mocked that to be born Bliss was enviable.

And here he was, fifty years old and the chairman of Bliss's, one of the most advanced department stores to be found in the provinces. 'Buy Bliss' was a ready-made slogan capable of infinite variation. 'Your Way to Bliss and Still More Bliss', urged spreads in the local press and posters on the huge plate-glass windows at strategic moments of the year. 'From Bliss to This', ran a particularly successful campaign one spring, showing the push-button ease and luxury that might be obtained in any home through wise purchasing and credit terms in the household departments. It coincided with a boom in local industry that heralded a wave of prosperity in the district. New three-piece suites and streamlined refrigerators became the local vogue, and it was a mark of failure in aspiring circles at that time not to refurbish the home in some way, however modest, even if only through the do-it-yourself department of Bliss's.

Exerting pressure to renew was the object of the campaign for March, or even earlier after a mild winter, when the first thin sunlight could be trusted to reveal the grime accumulated during the darker days and to arouse rest-lessness in average housewives. The prospering matron, making her after-the-sales forays into the better weather, must be lured into discontent with her faded curtains; she must be shown French silks, and the latest imports from Swedish glass factories. Mr. Bliss believed, naturally, in promoting British goods, but he had discovered long ago that the novelty of foreign design induced a reckless feeling of adventure, of cosmopolitan devil-may-care, in an otherwise phlegmatic customer. If a thing was British it was probably safe; but it might also be dull, reasoned the young-middle-aged matrons. Nothing foreign could possibly be uninteresting; its origin alone made it a talking-point.

Mr. Bliss enjoyed devising and implementing propaganda onslaughts upon the susceptibilities of his customers. There was a time and an opportunity for every approach. Concurrently with the spring-cleaning and refurnishing weeks, the Stork Bar ran a special line in prams and baby wear : each young mother who spent more than twenty pounds between certain dates was given a diminutive hairbrush, pink, blue or white, with, where known, the baby's name painted on it; and in cases of higher outlay there were further gifts. Experience had taught Mr. Bliss that the birth-rate leaped up in the weeks just before Budget Day. Modern couples not only got married at the time of year when it paid them best tax-wise, but planned their families with similar forethought. A mother who carried away a free hairbrush from Bliss's Stork Bar remained loyal for life; moving from nappies and plastic pants on to romper suits, schoolwear, Pre-Teens, and at last Young Sedgemouth, she found every-where the same concern that she should be a satisfied customer. As she grew plumper and more prosperous, she would branch forth into each department of the store : from pots and pans to cut-glass bowls, from brassière to neat fur toque, Bliss could supply almost her every need; from birth, in fact, to literally the grave. Second-genera-tion expectant mothers now bought layettes where, in the early post-war days, with clothes-coupons carefully counted, their own mothers had shopped for them; and old, valued customers, prompt payers of accounts, were qualifying for the last service that Mr. Bliss could give them, for he had bought up and absorbed as a going con-cern the best undertaking business in the town. Its former owner now had a post upon the board that directed, under the dictatorship of Mr. Bliss, the affairs of the store, and had proved a man of initiative with excellent ideas for enlarging the gardening section; it was, of course, in line with his own calling.

When the lease of the premises next door expired there was no limit to the expansion that might come if things worked out as Mr. Bliss intended. He dreamed of a multi-storey car-park linked to the main store by a sort of Bridge of Sighs, with lift service to all floors. It would come. With the magic of Bliss, all could be accomplished in time; this had been proved during the years, as Mr. Bliss climbed his chosen ladder, sometimes slowly, sometimes fast, but always ascending, swallowing on the way a neighbouring draper's and an inferior dress shop. The owners of these had been placed upon the board of Bliss's, where, grateful for solvency, they were perfect sycophants. Bertram reigned supreme. Only one of his aims remained impossible of fulfilment, and because he could not realise it, he rarely thought of it, dwelling instead on the magnitude of his achievements and searching for new targets.

Now it was October, and time to launch the Christmas campaign. Of all moments in the year, this was the season that Mr. Bliss most enjoyed. He loved the tinselly array in the window displays, the exotic novelties in the perfumery department with their tantalising feminine connotations, the piles of gay wrapping paper and glass baubles, the cards, the festive bedroom slippers and the glinting jewellery; and he loved the crowds, the press of bodies in the store as he strolled amid the aisles, a smiling pygmy giant who made all things possible for those with enough money to pay. The fame of Bliss had spread afar, and shoppers came from fifty miles away and more to browse among the merchandise.

In a few minutes the heads of departments and the window-dressers would enter Mr. Bliss's office, come by appointment to make final arrangements for the Yuletide Season, as Mr. Bliss liked to phrase it. The motif for the decorations this year was to be Biblical, with emphasis on the Three Wise Men. Mr. Bliss thought it time to underline the meaning of Christmas. Last year, to mark the cementing of new contracts for supplies from Scandinavia, the theme had been related to that area of the world, with Viking figures and laden long-ships featured in the windows. The year before, the store had become Aladdin's Cave, filled with tempting treasures; before that, the

Rainbow's End, with St. George triumphant by a brimming crock. Inspiration never seemed to fail.

Today's meeting would not last long, for policy had been decided weeks before and this was merely a final briefing, an exercise in harmonious delegation. We are all one big happy family, Mr. Bliss often said; he spared no pains to make this true, for a contented staff was an efficient one; disgruntled employees only gave poor service to the customer.

The chairman's office was large: between the desk and the doorway stretched a desert of pale grey carpet. The walls were papered with narrow silver stripes; several pastel paintings of vague flowers hung upon one, and, islanded starkly upon another, an example of modern surrealism in vivid hues. Two armchairs, severely contemporary, stood ready for important callers; a row of small, bowl-shaped seats, covered in brilliant tweeds, stretched from the door to the window. There was no outward sign of toil apart from the telephone and the intercom on the desk. Vital papers were put away; all the filing cabinets were clinically housed next door in the secretary's office.

She knocked. It was ten o'clock.

'Come in, Joan.'

'Your papers for the meeting, Mr. Bliss.'

Joan Seabright entered the room and laid a folder upon the blotting paper in front of Mr. Bliss.

'I hear them coming now,' she said.

There was, as she spoke, the sound of subdued voices in the passage, a female giggle, then a cough. Joan Seabright crossed the room and opened the door. First, four women dressed in bottle green filed in, then five men soberly arrayed in black suits, each with *Bliss* on a badge pinned to his lapel; at this store no customer was in any doubt as to who was one of them, and who was there to serve. These important persons, the heads of departments, were followed by the two window-dressers, both dressed in slacks and wearing soft slippers, with bright green nylon tunics, the colour of the Bliss delivery vans, cut with high necks like dentists' coats, and with a large embroidered *Bliss* aptly over the left breast.

The room became alive, expectant : there was a stir and a rustle as everyone sat down and assumed an air of more or less respectful attention. Mr. Bliss surveyed them all through his spectacles. Imperceptibly he inhaled; the atmosphere was filled with a pot-pourri of different odours ranging from Mr. Thomas's Three Nuns to Miss Westcott's Blue Grass. Young Mr. Jessamy from Household had recently adopted a tangy after-shave, and Sally Manners had sprayed her gorgeous auburn hair with a fragrant fixative. Mr. Bliss looked at her and sighed; he wished she would let it grow long, and hang silky and unfettered, like the dark locks of Wendy Brown, the other dresser. He must suggest it sometime; Sally would accept his counsel in the spirit it was given, that of a wise and kindly uncle. Perhaps he might even touch the disputed tresses, just gently, in a passing avuncular gesture, while they talked.

It was, at least, a thought to cherish.

He cleared his throat.

'Well, my friends,' he began.

2

After the meeting was over, Miss Westcott and Mr. Thomas went down the corridor, past the administrative offices where male and female clerks battled all day among ledgers and typewriters in a more sombre world than the departments of Bliss that were exhibited to the public, to the staff canteen. Here, over cigarettes and coffee, they would gravely discuss the prospects for the coming weeks; the wisdom or otherwise of the chairman's latest decrees; the health of Mr. Thomas's parrot and of Miss Westcott's ancient mother; the probable amount of this year's Christmas bonus; and other important matters.

The carpeted area of passage outside the executive offices merged into a lino-covered zone where the busy traffic of typists and accountants began. Here, the sound of footsteps never ceased, for someone was always on the way to somewhere else: girls to the cloakroom, or young men carrying mounds of paper darting from one doorway to another. As the two highly respected persons proceeded sedately along this thoroughfare, they caught glimpses of sloth and industry on either side: heads, dark or fair, bent over typewriters or adding machines; eyes, abstracted, gazed into space; and shapely forms clad in sweaters of all hues could be observed.

A plump, blonde girl hurried towards them as they made their stately progress, and with a wide grin, showing beautiful white teeth, flattened herself against the wall to let them pass. High round breasts thrust out her mauve turtle-neck sweater; a purple skirt finished not far below her hips; sturdy legs in white lacy tights ended in patent-sandalled feet. Mr. Thomas raised eyes to heaven in dismay at this vision, but Miss Westcott smiled.

'Good morning, Hermione,' she said. 'Thank you. dear.' Not all the girls would have stood aside in such seemly deference to seniority.

Hermione Tipps, a copy typist, pulled a face at Mr. Thomas's departing back, then stuck out her pert bust as she saw Mr. Jessamy further down the corridor by the lift. Too late: following the more senior gentlemen and the other ladies, he stepped within the cage and was borne away.

Descending in the lift, Paul Jessamy mourned, for Sally and Wendy had vanished into the tiny cell beside the stockrooms which was their headquarters. Here, the mighty heads of departments were obliged to wait upon them when they wanted special lines promoted. In a corner of the room lay a heap of pink naked plastic bodies, arms and legs detached from torsos, wigless heads piled on top, bundled together like the victims of some grisly massacre. More spare dummy models stood, ghost-like, shrouded in sheets in a large cupboard at one end of the room. Heaps of silver Christmas trees in various sizes, ordered for the use of different departments on their display counters, were stacked in a corner, branches still upthrust against their stems.

Sally perched on a high revolving stool at her drawing desk under the window and spun round several times, arms in the air.

'And so, my kiddy-winks, Christmas comes again, with all its seasonal extortion,' she cried. 'It gets earlier each year. God has spoken.'

'Sal, you are awful. I like Christmas. It gives you something to look forward to,' said Wendy.

'Hm. Well, it starts too soon. People don't want to think about it yet. The middle of November's time enough to start the fleecing.'

'Well, everyone else starts about now. Bliss's shouldn't lag behind,' said Wendy. 'The old man knows his stuff, you must admit.'

'I suppose so.' Sally sighed and picked up a piece of charcoal. 'What about these Kings, eh? Come and have a look at Balthazar.'

She began to draw swiftly on a sheet of rough paper. Under her skilful fingers a dramatic figure in flowing Eastern robes soon appeared. Wendy watched, her mane

14

of dark hair falling forward on either side of her thin face.

'You are clever, Sal,' she said, not for the first time. 'You're wasted here, really.'

Sally often thought so too. During her years in art school she had dreamed of being a dress designer, or at least a highly paid commercial artist wooed by the biggest advertising agencies in the land. Then her mother had fallen ill; after an operation she made a brief recovery, and Sally, knowing the bleak prognosis, had searched, at the end of her course, for a local post. At that time she could find nothing in the district where her training might be fully exploited; while she looked for something better, she took a temporary job at Bliss's, in the fashion department. Here, she showed such flair when she dressed some of the stands that her work was soon observed by the chairman on his daily round of the store. Mr. Bliss walked her through all the departments and prompted her to talk. It was she who transformed the very ordinary, rather folksy baby department into the Stork Bar; she designed and drew the nursery figures for the décor and found someone to take them; she painted the gay frieze.

Until this time the windows of the store had been adequately, but not inspiringly, dressed by two girls who worked under the guidance of the departments whose goods were to be shown. Mr. Bliss had little difficulty in gradually creating for Sally her present post. Miss West-cott gave her a free hand with the fashion windows; the contrast between these and those on either side was so pronounced that the board unanimously recognised her talents and she found herself appointed to the newly created position of head display designer, with the two previous dressers as her helpers. One of these soon left to have a baby; the second, Wendy, worked cheerfully on with Sally in happy and unambitious partnership. Sally never intended to stay, but before she could escape the net closed round her. Her mother died, and her father, desolate, needed her. She promised herself that in a year or so, when she had got him going on his own, she would leave and go to London. That was three years ago, and she saw no prospect now of breaking free.

'We could open our own boutique,' Wendy said. She scooped up some of the arms and legs that lay piled upon the floor. 'You'd design the dresses, and I'd make them up. We'd be like Mary Quant in no time.'

'We might at that.' Sally laid Balthazar on one side and began on Caspar. The figures, when they reached their final form, would be graphed out and expanded to near life size, then drawn on hardboard to make firm models for display. Each window, travelling round the store from west to east, would describe a further movement in the journey to the Star which would be in position above the main entrance. 'But how could we abandon poor Babs? We'd break his heart.'

'We'd break his bank, more likely, winning trade away,' said Wendy. 'Imagine setting up as his rivals.'

'Imagine it, yes,' said Sally. Sometimes she thought she was doomed for ever to have Mr. Bliss appearing by her side whenever she emerged from the lift, or left the canteen, or entered her office with a pile of samples. They met quite often enough for her in the normal course of duty, since they conferred at least once a week about future plans. But Sally was not ungrateful; her job was well paid, and had prestige and privileges; it was often interesting, and her own talent had created a certain indispensability.

Paul Jessamy stood sadly in the descending lift, paying no heed to the talk of his colleagues. At each floor, one or another got out, until only he was left, riding on in lonely silence to the basement. He wished now that he had followed Miss Westcott and Mr. Thomas to the cafeteria; but he had been buoyed up with hope that Sally would be coming down too. He might have known that she

16

would go straight to that office of hers, that retreat where he seldom had a genuine excuse for calling. If ever he managed to dredge one up, he would stand, gawky and awkward, on the threshold of the room, a very different figure indeed from the normally assured, even suave young head of the household and furnishing departments.

The atmosphere below street level was calm and hushed; gone was the flurry of the ground-floor traffic; down here, people browsed at leisure. No one bought a sofa in a hurry; there was no atmosphere of urgency in this region. Walking through, Paul paused to move fractionally a yellow-covered easy chair; he flicked an invisible speck of dust from a Scandinavian coffee table.

In Lighting, Mildred Smith seemed to be in trouble: after a moment's distant observation he saw that she could not find the pair to a lampshade held by a customer who looked impatient. Paul smoothly intervened, found the missing partner sandwiched in a stack of another design, and made a mental note to cause fresh stocks to be fetched from upstairs. Mildred, red-faced, concentrated on her customer. It would happen that Mr. Jessamy had caught her in a difficulty; another minute, and she would have found the shade herself. She set her lips defiantly and looked expectantly at her customer, who now stood, a shade in either hand, musing on their merits. Mildred had already found five other assorted pairs for her to try, and arranged them on different lampstands so that she might see the effect. Very likely the woman would leave in the end with nothing. She waited, mutinous, and was proved right.

'I'll think about it.'

The woman handed Mildred back the shades, put on her leather gloves, and walked away.

Furious, Mildred picked up the rejected shades. She longed to fling them after the retreating back of the customer. With a mighty effort she pulled herself together and began to pile the shades methodically in place so that she would not get caught out again.

'Have you had your coffee yet, Miss Smith?'

Paul had appeared once more behind her. It was fortunate that she was discovered being conscientious.

'No, Mr. Jessamy.' Her voice was muffled, her face hidden as she bent over her stocks.

'Well, you go off now. We don't seem busy. I'll put the rest of those shades away,' said Paul.

Mildred rose obediently.

'Shall I fetch some more of those pink ones, like that woman wanted to see, while I'm upstairs?' she offered.

'Yes, please.' Paul was surprised at this show of initiative on the part of Miss Smith. She was for ever in a muddle with her wares; he rescued her when he could, for he knew that she was a willing, well-intentioned girl, but it was clear that her heart was not in Lighting.

As Mildred departed Mr. Bliss stepped from the background where, unseen, he had observed this interlude.

'How is Miss Smith getting on?' he asked.

Paul was undismayed at being discovered doing the work of his junior assistant. He piled three cream damask shades into a cone.

'She's a good worker, she tries hard,' he said. 'She's just had one of those customers who want to see everything and go off with nothing.'

'Very irritating,' said Mr. Bliss.

'Well, she'll have to get used to it. It happens all the time,' said Paul.

'True, true. But I wonder if she'd do better somewhere else. In Toiletries, perhaps. She seems an inartistic type of girl, but most young women are interested in cosmetics. Someone aware of the visual appeal of lamps and lighting might be more use to you.'

'Well, yes.' Paul was relieved that Mildred was not in peril of dismissal.

'We could do some moving round. Mrs. Betts is looking rather tired; you know her, do you? She might find it easier down here.'

Paul did remember a thin, pale woman he had seen looking singularly out of place among the bright aids to beauty she sought to sell.

'She's a pleasant woman,' Mr. Bliss was saying. 'Things are difficult at home, I believe.'

'So I understand.'

Paul lived in the same street as Mrs. Betts; he sometimes met her husband in The Bell, and did not like what he had seen of him. Peter Betts was often offensive and quarrelsome. And the young son and daughter had pinched, nervous expressions contrasting with the rosy faces of most of the children to be seen in the district.

'It might suit her much better here,' Paul added, realising how tranquil it could often be, and how much space there was. In Toiletries the gangways were narrow and it was always crowded.

'I'll look into it,' Mr. Bliss said. 'Any other problems?'

'No, sir.'

'Well, now. How about those new pottery bases we ordered from Wales. Do you think they'll go?' Mr. Bliss switched from staff to goods, and Paul responded. They talked for a few minutes about various lines, moving down the carpeted aisles among the merchandise. Eventually, with a nod, Mr. Bliss moved on. Walking on the balls of his feet to appear taller, with his hands clasped behind his back, he proceeded towards the stairs that led to the mezzanine, where was the burgeoning garden department.

Paul watched him go. No one knew where his daily tour would start, or when it would be. He was liable to pop up at any moment, anywhere in the store. It was disconcerting, but effective. There was no doubt that he knew an almost uncomfortable amount about everyone who worked for him. The proposed exchange of Mrs. Betts for Mildred was inspired: had the old man planned it in advance, or did he dream it up when he saw Mildred at a loss? Paul was certain he had witnessed the whole incident and only waited to reveal himself when it was over.

He deserves that house on Castle Hill, Paul thought. He doesn't miss a trick.

Overhead, Mr. Bliss moved lightly through the garden spades, the barrows and the bulbs; this section would disappear for the Christmas season, giving up its place to cards and wrappings. When spring came it would expand. He accelerated as he came to the last flight of stairs leading into Haberdashery. Here on the ground floor, apart from Baggage in one corner and Fabric Fair at the back of the store, no male assistant was to be found. Here, behind the glass-fronted counters, among the ribbons and the belts, the powder and the scent, the stockings and the gloves, was a world of women. Nostrils slightly flared, Mr. Bliss stepped forth.

3

High up on Castle Hill, overlooking the town, Shirley Bliss sat by her picture window gazing at the view, which today was mist-dimmed and bleak. She had seen it so often, in all weathers, at all seasons and all hours, that there was nothing new to notice.

She was bored.

On her knee was a new novel, in its shiny wrapper, collected this morning from the library. In spite of the blurb which claimed it to be a tale of absorbing passion and suspense, it failed to grip her. A box of chocolate creams rested on the arm of her chair; automatically she took one out and put it in her mouth. After some minutes more of blank, unthinking existence, she sighed, took up her book, and began again to read, but with no more success. She looked at her watch. Three o'clock. Almost three hours before she might expect Bertie home.

She discarded the book and picked up a magazine. It was full of Christmas propaganda, selections and advice. She had already made her lists and chosen her cards. Everything would soon arrive, sent direct from the wholesaler, with no more effort from her. She would at least be able to occupy an hour or two gift-wrapping the parcels and addressing the cards. She could even spend time going into town to select coloured paper, ribbon and tags. Bertie would, of course, bring her back a choice collection of all these things if she asked him; but to go and choose them herself would be something to do. Perhaps Bertie would take her lunch at The Star, and in the afternoon she might go to the cinema. She began to cheer up at the prospect of filling a day.

Shirley had met Bertram soon after Dunkirk, when he was a lieutenant in the R.A.S.C. and stationed nearby while his unit re-formed. He had come into her father's ironmonger's shop to buy a pair of garden secateurs for his mother's birthday, and Shirley, newly grown-up with her dark hair in a sleek page-boy style, the current fashion, had served him. They met again a week later at a dance in aid of the Red Cross. At first Bertram, encountering her face-to-face in a Paul Jones, had not remembered where he had seen the plump, shy girl with the large brown eyes; but Shirley, who recognised him at once, had artlessly reminded him. Afterwards she considered it miraculous that she had gone to the dance at all : she had set forth apprehensively with three other girls who all hoped to meet, if not their fate, at least adventure; Shirley merely aspired not to be a wallflower all the evening. In Bertram's eyes her chief merit was that she was shorter than he; for this reason alone he danced with her several times and offered, half-heartedly, to see her home. She lived with her parents in a stucco villa, creeper-clad, on the edge of the town, in a district favoured by tradesmen and bank clerks. Bertram discovered, as they walked through the dark, deserted streets, that her father owned the ironmonger's where he had met her, and that she was his only child. She had been sent away from home to an expensive boarding school where she had learned very little and developed a loathing for organised games. Her father, whose ambition for her knew no limit, had planned to send her abroad to learn languages and social grace; the war put paid to this plan, and Shirley came down from the heights to the counter at Hawkins'. During the years when she was away at school she lost contact with her local childhood friends; she was just beginning to pick up the threads of Sedgemouth life again when Bertram appeared. A week after the dance he took her to the cinema and held her hand during *Wuthering Heights,* throughout which she softly wept. Three months later they were married, she in white crêpe, the only fabric from which it seemed possible to make dresses in those days, with a long tulle veil and her cousin Esme as a bridesmaid. A photograph of this event stood on the walnut bureau in the room where Shirley now sat. Her face, round and unlined, gazed from the silver frame beside Bertram's pleased smile. Harry Hawkins, resplendent in his hired morning suit, and Shirley's frail, thin mother flanked them on either side. In the background stood Bertram's mother, still a part-time piano teacher but living now in the country, with a garden where she grew prize roses and sweet peas. Bride and groom had left by train for a brief honeymoon in Devon, where it rained every day. To Shirley the surrender of her virginity was a symbolic act, painful beyond anticipation but unshrinkingly endured; Bertram, inexperienced but determined, to his own surprise discovered tenderness. Two weeks later he sailed for the Middle East to become part of the Eighth Army. Shirley continued to work at the shop as before, her status altered but her life unchanged.

Bertram returned after over four years, a little more lined and a good deal more assured, and a major to boot. As soon as he was demobilised he joined his father-in-law in the business, which soon began to grow and prosper. The young couple moved into a small house bought for them by Shirley's father. Shirley stayed on in her job, where she now did the book-keeping and ordering; she had become very competent. She intended to leave as soon as she expected a child, but this moment never came. The months ran on into years, and with unfailing regularity she was disappointed. The doctor whom, in a burst of desperate courage, she consulted, could find nothing wrong; he counselled patience and perseverance. Life went on; she was always busy, and considered herself happy enough. Bertram and her father worked very hard in those early years; Hawkin's Hardware started to expand, acquired extra space, and became the limited company of Hawkins and Bliss: Bertram saw his war gratuity multiply several times. The shop began to stock china and glass as the white wartime utility designs were superseded; Shirley started a knitting-wool and haberdashery counter, and then a baby department. She still expected to rock a cradle of her own, but meanwhile she helped to trim and equip those of other women.

In the evening, when they went home, she never failed to cook Bertram an excellent meal; her culinary ability increased with the lessening of food restrictions: she enjoyed good food herself and was willing to take trouble preparing it. Because she worked all day in the shop, Bertram thought it right to help her in the house; at weekends he cleaned windows and gardened, peeled potatoes and washed up. They had plenty of joint interests; there was the business, which they shared, to talk about, with increasing problems as it grew. Good staff was hard to find; when discovered, it must be kept. Potential lines of development had to be decided. Soon, space or the lack of it was the chief restriction to their expansion. Every corner and cranny of the old-fashioned building was filled to capacity; furniture in one section; down half a flight of stairs and up a ramp into bed-linen; along a narrow corridor into glass and china. A subterranean passageway through the cellar linked the original hardware department with umbrellas and leather goods. Customers jostled against one another in the cramped aisles and passages; the assistants grew weary tramping up and down stairs and struggling with stock in the confined spaces, but because of a generous bonus scheme introduced at Bertram's suggestion they were uncomplaining.

Then disaster struck. One night the shop caught fire. The blaze swept rapidly through the whole place and gutted it. Shirley's father, standing in the middle of the charred shell, felt it was the end of his life's work. To survive the war without being bombed and then by an accident to lose everything seemed too unjust. The cause of the fire was never discovered.

But while Mr. Hawkins and Shirley, stunned, grieved together, Bertram exulted. He saw at once that it would be possible, when the insurance claim was met, to build in the place of an old-fashioned, inconvenient huddle of buildings, a co-ordinated, well-planned block. He was indefatigable, fighting for their just recompense and then hounding the authorities for planning consent. He badgered the architect and the builders, getting estimate and counter-estimate and finally almost laying each concrete slab in place himself in his efforts to hasten the proceedings. At last, phoenix-like, rose the new Bliss's.

It had to be Bliss's. Mr. Hawkins never got over the shock of the fire and he died before the new building was finished. Shirley's mother lived on for another eighteen months. Shirley, whose job at the shop ceased with the fire, was fully occupied caring for her parents. After her father's death her mother came to live with her and Bertram. By the time she, too, died, Shirley had almost lost touch with the store. While the rebuilding was going on Bertram travelled abroad to explore marketing and presentation as carried out in other countries; he was much impressed with Scandinavian design and production, and this was how his link with these countries began. Shirley found, when free at last from the claims of her parents, that the whole enterprise had grown too big for her to recognise. Even the faces were new. Most of the former staff had found other jobs, but Miss Westcott and Mr. Thomas had both asked to return. Bertram had acquired a secretary whose poise and efficiency were such that so lowly a title seemed an inadequate description of her post; she was a brisk, smart divorcée busy putting two sons through school and university.

The new shop prospered. Bertram was quick to discard unprofitable lines and pursue better ones; he had the true Midas touch. Soon the store was extended at the back, above the yard where lorries unloaded. After this, two neighbouring shops were bought up; each time Bertram swallowed a business, the victim was grateful, for it was surrender or die.

Shirley no longer needed to count the cost of her housekeeping. She learned to drive and had her own small car; she had a mink coat, which she seldom wore.

The Blisses had moved out to Castle Hill three years ago, into a house that had been designed especially for them. It was long and low, built of brick with cedar facing, and it had oil-fired heating, indirect lighting, huge windows, and polished stairs rising like a ladder from the well of the hall, forever making Shirley nervous that her foot would slip between the treads. She missed, though she never dared say so, the dark, friendly muddle of the glory-hole under the stairs where they had lived before, where she kept the vacuum cleaner and the flower vases in a huddle among spare light bulbs, a hammer and the pliers. Now there was a special cupboard to house the cleaning equipment, as large as a small room, and places for spare bulbs and tools, and a flower room. There was too much space. Pale carpets stretched across the floors; long, pleated curtains draped the wide windows; angular but extremely comfortable modern furniture in colour combinations Shirley would never have chosen was placed about the house. She and Bertram slept in a vast great bed, feet apart from one another, with an apricot padded headboard bracketing them at one end. Their kitchen, yellow and black, had a breakfast bar stretched across the centre and the very latest automatic self-timing cooker. Shirley was sometimes afraid of all her appliances, which occasionally went wrong. Life was much simpler in the old days; it wasn't as if she had a family of youngsters to keep the washing-machine turning and to eat pastry made with her mixer and watched as it baked through a glass oven door. All this seemed excessive just for Bertie and herself. But it was very comfortable : there was space for all her clothes, of which she had plenty, for Bertie encouraged her to dress expensively, saying it advertised his success. Likewise, the house was a permanent display of what might be bought at the store : Bertie already talked of changing the rose silk living-room curtains which Shirley liked for a new abstract print that had caught his fancy. At intervals they entertained to dinner the people whom Bertram sought to impress : the mayor, or leading members of the town council and their wives; his bank manager; other prosperous tradesmen.

Shirley polished and cleaned and cooked; she tried to

expend on the house the energy that previously she had put into the whole of life, with her work in the shop and in the little box-like house where they had lived for so long, but there was Mrs. Phillips each day to thwart her. Besides, Shirley had slowed up. Always plump, she was now almost fat; most of her clothes were made for her these days. Her eyes were still large, but her face was faintly florid and her once dark, shining hair was streaked with grey. She wore it drawn into a soft chignon which became her but was unfashionable and made hats difficult; Bertie considered she should always wear a hat in Sedgemouth. Under the burden of her excess weight, her ankles and feet often swelled as she bustled about inventing tasks to fill up her day. She punctuated the hours with little meals: tea on waking, then coffee and toast for breakfast; more coffee at eleven and a biscuit or two. Lunch, then tea later on, and finally chocolates till Bertie came home. After that, sherry tided her over till dinner. She sometimes had cocoa at bedtime.

Shirley had joined the Townswomen's Guild and a floral artistry group; she was not greatly stirred by the activities of the Guild; but she enjoyed the flower arranging and had a gift for it, though she often felt ill at ease among the ladies from the country villages around who formed most of the association. They lived mainly in venerable stone houses with acres of garden and had daughters with ponies or problems, and sons who suffered from acne and were struggling for university places; she felt alien, though recognised by all as one of the most skilful of the group. Because she lacked children, she lacked too a common passport into communication; even her neighbours on Castle Hill had difficult long-haired sons or mini-skirted daughters. For a time Shirley had a King Charles spaniel, but he was run over and she did not replace him; she had not really loved him.

When she felt restless and sad she rebuked herself, for

she had everything a woman could want except for a family. She forgot that it was her own father's prosperous business that had made Bertie's empire possible, and that her hard work in the early years had provided free and capable help when it was most needed. There was nothing now to occupy her mind except Bertie and his welfare; she could look forward only to getting slower on her feet and fatter still, becoming even more dependent on the comforts of life with which she was surrounded, and less able to find resources within herself.

On some distant day she supposed Bertie would retire, though she could not imagine it. To whom would he hand over? And what would he do with himself? When it was no longer necessary for him to help about the house in his spare time he resumed a boyhood hobby and had become a keen philatelist. Stamp-collecting was now his only interest outside the store; he brooded nightly over his treasures, and corresponded about the globe, swopping and completing sets. His collection was quite valuable. Still, he could scarcely turn it into a full-time occupation for his old age.

She supposed that in fact nothing would change. He would crawl to the store if he had to get there in an invalid chair, until he died.

And who would take over then? There was no nephew or niece on either side of the family.

Shirley riffled through the magazine. There was an article describing how to arrange two poinsettias and some holly in a copper bowl with a tall red candle in the centre for a Christmas decoration. She read it painstakingly, her eye travelling slowly along each line, taking in every recommendation from how to cut the stems to how they should be secured, in a nest of crumpled wire netting anchored with plasticene. On the next page tempting colour spreads illustrated rich fruit cakes and spicy festive dishes, with recipes superimposed. She scrutinised these in detail. Bertram might like the cinnamon pudding, she thought, mentally savouring it as she translated the ingredients into an image of the finished concoction. She took scissors from a drawer of the chest, cut out the page, replaced the scissors, and then went to the kitchen where she inserted her cutting into a snap folder already crammed with similar trophies culled from magazines and newspapers through the years. She was always trying out new dishes on Bertram; he professed to prefer cheese and biscuits to puddings, but she loved pastry and cakes and often treated herself to a scone or a piece of fruit pie at idle moments in the day.

She decided to indulge herself now. She put on the kettle, then laid a tray neatly with cup, saucer and milk jug, and saccharin tablets in a small porcelain snuff box, Bertie's present on her last birthday. Her one genuine concession to weight-watching was abstention from sugar in the raw, though she ate a good deal of it disguised in the pies and the soufflés she consumed. When the kettle boiled she made tea in a small, flowered pot, put two scones and a piece of iced coffee cake on a plate, and carried her little repast through to the living-room.

Eating it took some time. She drank two cups of sweet tea. Then she looked at her watch. She had succeeded in occupying most of the afternoon. Bertie would be home in less than two hours.

She went out to the kitchen again, put her used cup, saucer and plate in the dishwasher and washed up the tea-pot and spoon. Then she began to assemble the constituents for dinner that Mrs. Phillips had earlier prepared. Potatoes and sprouts were ready in their pans; soup had been made; there was a fruit flan in the larder. Shirley pottered about putting the chicken on its spit ready to roast and getting out dishes and plates. She managed to spin out her preparations through a further half-hour. Then she went upstairs and changed from her rust-coloured tweed suit into a brown jersey dress with a velvet collar. She powdered her round, red cheeks, carefully blued her eyelids and mascaraed her lashes. Her pale, full lips she covered afresh with dark red lipstick. Round her neck she fastened a triple row of cultured pearls, Bertie's gift on their twentieth anniversary. They rested in proud echelon on the pigeon plateau of her breasts. Finally she exchanged her brown lizard low-heeled shoes for a pair of patent leather, easing her small, neat feet carefully into them, and then went downstairs again.

The living-room was immaculately tidy; it was never otherwise. A large bowl of rose-tinged chrysanthemums, beautifully arranged, that picked up the colour of the curtains, stood on a corner shelf. The chair covers were smooth and unshrunken. She sat down in her usual place on the deep sofa, sinking back against the cushions and easing her heels out of her shoes. All was ready for the return of the master.

4

This week the windows of Bliss's were dressed in autumnal shades of brown and deepest red. Fabrics in these hues, printed and plain, were draped fanwise like bridal trains, flowing over a chocolate-coloured carpet; and plastic ladies wore fashions in these shades.

Sally had been satisfied with this display when first she set it up. Its hint of fading foliage led naturally towards the fact of winter. Now, though, she was bored with it, and eager to get on with the next theme, in black and white. Later, as Christmas approached, there would be gift suggestions piled on layers of crimson velvet, artificial trees, shiny baubles and billowing ribbon bows. At this moment she was busy assembling an army of Eastern potentates cut out of hardboard and mounted on firm bases; several times over, the Three Wise Men, in various poses and nearly life size, reclined against the walls of her office, waiting to receive their final touches.

'About December the first for you, fellow,' she said, slapping an extra curl on to a luxuriant beard.

'Babs will never leave it so long. He'll want them out next week, see if he doesn't,' said Wendy. She wore a paint-bedaubed smock, and, wielding a large brush, was filling in an expanse of Balthazar's robe in deep purple. 'He's packed with Christmas spirit already. Any minute now he'll be lying in wait for you with a sprig of mistletoe.'

'He doesn't need mistletoe. All he wants is opportunity.' Sally emphasised an eyebrow with a firm stroke.

'Dirty old man,' Wendy pronounced.

'Oh, he's just male,' Sally said. 'Maybe Shirley-wirley doesn't cater for his demands.'

'What do you think they are? Flagellation?' Wendy began to giggle.

'Maybe. Or boots. Imagine Shirley striding round starkers but for thigh-length suède jobs. With her hair let down and reaching to her navel.'

They started to chortle.

'It wouldn't reach so far.'

'Well, to her withers, then.'

'Where on earth are they?'

'Here, on a horse.' Sally waved at the back of her neck with her brush and a blob of paint landed on her own hair.

'Idiot.' Wendy put down her own brush and came to the rescue with a piece of rag. They were both overcome with mirth and sat giggling helplessly for some minutes, their work forgotten. Sally knew that without these occa-

31

sional moments of lunacy which they shared she would often have found the days unbearably tedious; she feared sometimes that she was responsible for a grave decline in the level of Wendy's thinking during the years of their partnership.

'Poor old Shirley. She's too nice really to make fun of,' said Sally. 'I don't envy her lot.'

'Nor I. He's a nasty old lecher,' said Wendy.

'Be fair, Miss Brown. Has he ever laid a finger on you, may I ask?' Sally demanded.

'No fear. It's you he's after, remember,' said Wendy. 'Watch out.'

'In fact, he wouldn't dare try anything on,' said Sally. 'He's got too much regard for his reputation. Think of the scandal! "Young shop assistant screams for help as chairman ravishes her!" Can't you see the headlines? You know, I almost despise him more for holding back than if he had a go. To dream, but not to do.' She stood back, squinting at Melchior, who in turn gazed earnestly into the distance.

'Well, one can't just go around giving in to one's impulses without a thought,' Wendy pointed out reasonably. 'We'd soon be in gaol.'

'Would we? Do you long for some illegal thing?'

'Of course. A chinchilla coat and a diamond ring,' said Wendy promptly. 'But suppose he did make a pass, you know, and one resisted. Would one get the sack, I wonder? It could be very embarrassing.'

'Not half as embarrassing as if one hadn't resisted,' said Sally. 'Think of it, next day. He's repellent. I can't think why Shirley dotes on him so. She's far too good for him.'

'Yes, she's a dear,' Wendy agreed. 'I don't suppose she has a clue, really.'

'You mean about his base, secret nature and lascivious thoughts?' Sally pondered. 'Maybe she's busy having an affair herself with the man who mends the telly, or something.'

'Not she. She has eyes only for Babs,' declared Wendy.

'You're right, really. She doesn't know what she's missing in the wider world,' Sally said.

'Talking of eyes,' Wendy went on, laying down her brush and scratching her nose. 'What are you going to do about sheep's-eyes Paul?'

'Oh, goodness knows. Wouldn't you like him?' Sally gave Melchior's grey eyebrows an extra interrogative twirl.

'I don't want your cast-offs, thanks very much,' said Wendy. 'I'll find my own material, fresh and unspoiled.'

'How awful that sounds.' Sally shuddered. 'Green and callow. Give me a bit of experience every time.' She moved Melchior to one side; he was complete. Another figure, arms outstretched pointing the way to the gift boutique, waited to be painted.

'Are you going to London this weekend?'

It was not a disconnected remark. Whenever Sally's free Saturday came round she went away for the weekend, telling her father that she was visiting a school-friend; but Wendy knew where, in fact, she really went.

'I suppose so.' Sally ran a hand through her short hair, making it stand on end in a manner that Mr. Bliss would certainly have found provocative.

'You don't sound very keen. Why not give it up?' Wendy said, greatly daring.

Sally occasionally, after these weekends, revealed despair.

'I can't,' she said.

'You'd find someone else.'

'Who? Paul, the faithful? Don't make me laugh. I think even Babs might be better than that doe-eyed spaniel,' said Sally, with a fine flourish of metaphor. 'Maybe I'll encourage him with a wicked leer next time we're alone in the lift, and see where it leads. He wouldn't know how to make the next move, I bet.' Neatly she turned the conversation, and the two girls were laughing when the door opened a few minutes later and in came Mr. Bliss himself, the target of their humour.

Bertram scrutinised the figures they were completing, making small approving sounds. As he bent over Melchior, Wendy suddenly realised that the two faces were identical: if Bertram were to grow a grey beard and bushy brows they would be twins. How slow she had been not to see it before; of course this was a typical way for Sally to divert herself. She was convulsed with suppressed giggles while Sally stood gravely beside Mr. Bliss and his double. Wendy was so much overcome that it was some seconds before she could pull herself together enough to listen to the chairman's words. She became aware that he was following his commendations of their labours with remarks about the store's Christmas party, to be held early in January. The weeks before Christmas and the chaos of the sale period immediately following were judged by Bertram not to be a suitable time for this junketing, but he thought it invigorated everyone in the doldrum days that came before spring could be heralded in a tumult of yellow and green. He was urging both girls to be present at all costs. You put up a black if you stayed away, but it was rather a drag. The same old faces that you saw every day surrounded you. If a new one were to be seen it had been brought by a colleague and was, therefore, as you might say, already spoken for. There was no future to be found at a Bliss celebration.

'I'm not sure of my plans,' Sally was hedging. 'My father may have made some arrangement.'

'But I hope you will bring him too, Sally,' said Bertram. 'He would enjoy the evening, I'm sure. Why don't you both dine with us first? My wife will be delighted. And Wendy too?' He turned to her, enchanted by the inspiration he had just conceived. Annually the dinner guests included his fellow directors and their wives, and Miss Westcott and Mr. Thomas, none of whom were remarkable for their vivacity. This time a dash of youth would be most agreeable.

Wendy, caught unawares, goggled.

'If you have not already invited a partner, Wendy, may I suggest Paul Jessamy?' went on Bertram, suavely.

When Wendy still did not utter, he nodded. 'I'll arrange it with him,' he said, and went away.

Left alone, the girls gaped at each other.

'Well,' said Sally. 'God has spoken.'

'It'll be fun to see Bliss Castle,' said Wendy, referring to the house by its irreverent nickname. It was in fact called Cedar Grange. 'And Paul will be thrilled to bits, even though he's lumbered with me instead of you. We can swop, anyway. I think your dad's a doll.'

'Babs certainly means to be sure of us, fixing the date so far in advance,' said Sally grimly. She thought of Derek: what if he could escape that night? She hated being pinned down weeks ahead by other people.

She said aloud, 'Let's give Babs time to get out of the way and then go for coffee. I'm parched after that little lot.'

Alone in the lift, travelling down to the basement, Bertram Bliss wove a fantasy about the night of the dance. Sally, wearing black velvet which clung to her curves and showed off her creamy skin, would arrive early at Cedar Grange with her father. He would ply them both with cocktails. Shirley, whose costume he did not trouble to invent, would entertain the parent while he conducted the daughter on a tour of the house. This inspection would take some time; meaningfully they would loiter here and there. Reluctantly they would return to the claims of the other guests. Later, in the ballroom of The Star, where the event was annually held, they would dance together to the stimulating beat of the Rocketeers; their bodies would touch, their hands would be clasped, her cheek would rest against his shoulder, his lips be near her flame-coloured hair. In his euphoric condition Bertram overlooked the fact that this would be a feat indeed, since she was by several inches the taller. He would persuade Shirley to leave the dance before the evening ended; her feet always gave out early anyway, and she tended to grow flushed and sleepy in the hot atmosphere. Mr. Manners should be granted the privilege of escorting her home, and this would automatically ensure that to Bertram fell the duty of taking Sally to her door. The Rover would purr silently through the streets and out to Warren End, where the Manners lived on the opposite side of the town from Castle Hill. He was just mentally switching off the engine and enfolding Sally's complaisant form in his embrace when the lift stopped and he was obliged to step out among a forest of oak ladderback chairs which Paul Jessamy was arranging.

Paul was delighted with the dinner invitation, when after a long business discussion it was given. He managed to ignore the fact that Wendy was to be his partner, for Sally would at least be there, and work-wise it could only advance him to fraternise socially with Mr. Bliss. Paul knew his own value; he was the youngest of the male department heads, and in the normal expectancy of such things had accordingly several useful decades of work before him. With his experience, if he were to move to London, or to one of the big groups of stores, he would certainly prosper; but he wanted to stay here, where living was pleasant, the country at the door and the coast not far away. True, there was winter to take heed of, as now, when his boat was perforce laid up; but summer would come again, the *Mary Lou* would take the water once more, and who could tell? Sally might change her mind and come with him as crew, as she had done before, in the summer of last year.

He came back to dry land with a jolt.

'Mrs. Betts?' Mr. Bliss had mentioned her name. Paul's subconscious registered the question, and he replied promptly. 'She's settling down nicely, sir. Seems happy to be here. Would you like a word with her?'

Together they walked to the electrical department. There, illumined by the glow of many lamps, Marjorie Betts could be observed showing marble bases to a stout woman in a sheepskin coat and boots, with a sheepskin hat on her head and a face not unlike a ewe. Mrs. Betts was being pleasant and competent. They watched her carry two bases to her desk and make out an order for their delivery; she had made a good sale.

'Carry on, Paul. I'll speak to her when she's free,' said Mr. Bliss.

Marjorie Betts did not notice his approach. She was busy recording the details of the recent transaction in her sales book, and calculating the amount of her commission. Already she was doing better here than she had among the cosmetics, and her feet no longer ached.

'Well, Mrs. Betts, settling down all right, are you?'

Mr. Bliss was swaying to and fro on his heels, watching her with that penetrating look that the girls upstairs all giggled about. To Mrs. Betts, his interest seemed kindness unparalleled.

'Oh, yes, thank you, Mr. Bliss.'

'No problems?'

'No, thank you. Mr. Jessamy has shown me everything most carefully.' She looked anxious for a moment; perhaps she had made some mistake.

Bertram was quick to sense her apprehension.

'He tells me you are getting on splendidly,' he said encouragingly, and saw her relax. She still seemed extremely tense, despite her release from the pressures of the busy toiletry department.

'How are the children? Looking forward to Christmas, I expect.'

'Oh yes. Children always do, don't they?' Marjorie's face softened a little at this domestic note.

'Let's see, how old are they now?' Mr. Bliss prompted.

'Amanda's twelve and Michael's ten,' she said.

'Of course. And both doing well, I'm sure,' Mr. Bliss said. 'We must tempt at least one of them to join us, later on.'

'Oh!' Marjorie gasped. She had not thought of such a thing. Vague castles-in-the-air about university or teacher-training came sometimes to her mind when she thought about the future, but sheer survival now took all her energy.

Mr. Bliss decided not to enquire about the well-being of Mr. Betts. He must do some research to discover the true position there.

'Well, let me know if you have any difficulties,' he said, smiled again, and left.

Marjorie watched him go. Her heart beat fast with nervous excitement. She knew he meant what he said; several of the older members of the staff had been helped through various crises not only with advice, but with loans and extra leave. The young ones might mock, but time would teach them what was valuable and how lucky they were to work for someone who put so much effort into ensuring their welfare.

She wondered if she would ever find the courage to take her troubles up to his office on the top floor, and how he would counsel her if he knew all that went on at Number 65, The Grove.

5

Shirley backed her scarlet Mini out of the garage, swung round in a wide arc on the asphalt in front of the house, and set off down Castle Hill towards Sedgemouth. Her way went past large, pleasant houses with well-ordered gardens; then, gradually, the houses began to diminish in size and huddle closer together as she approached the town, until finally they became continuous rows of buildings. She crossed the bridge over the river : now the traffic was dense, with cars, lorries and buses filling the streets as she drew nearer to the centre. She never had to face the problem of where to park, which was becoming increasingly acute for the average motorist as the town grew; traffic wardens, grim in their yellow-banded caps and sweeping mackintoshes, harried them ceaselessly. But Shirley drove straight to the yard at the back of Bliss's and tucked her little car in behind Bertram's Rover. She went into the store by the goods entrance, and at once felt stimulated by the familiar smell of straw and sacking in the unpacking department, where quiet, overalled figures were undoing crates of glass and china, and stacking newly arrived furniture. The men looked up and nodded at her as she passed. She hurried through. Once, she would never have passed without a word with each of them, but Bertram had several times caught her chatting and hinted that time cost money, so now she walked straight on, up the stairs, panting a little, and through the staff door into the basement.

She strolled around. Paul Jessamy certainly knew his job, if it was he who had devised these layouts of chairs and tables. Everything was arranged so as to tempt the passer-by to linger and look, even to pause and sit for a moment. There were groups of customers doing both, she noticed, and saw Paul busy with a distinguished-looking grey-haired man who seemed to be buying a leather arm-chair. Many of the wealthier people in the area, Shirley knew, admitted only antique pieces into their homes and would be aghast at the suggestion that they should buy dining tables or chests of drawers in a modern store; but even they, on occasion, needed sofas and armchairs and did not always want to repose themselves on Victorian resurrections.

She wandered through Kitchenware, where bright copper pans and enamelled French casseroles made splashes of colour among the conventional aluminium, then up to the mezzanine floor where the garden depart-ment had by this time made way for Christmas cards and wrapping paper. She browsed among the cards, wishing now that she had chosen a comic one of Father Christmas coasting across the sky while an assortment of his cus-tomers waited expectantly below, rather than the holly and Christmas roses painted on a white ground which was in fact her selection for this year. But Bertie did not approve of whimsy. He had a long list of compulsory cards to send from the store, apart from their private one; busi-ness connections expected it, and a large, magnificent card was annually arranged for by Joan, who usually chose a reproduction of an old print, or a Peter Scott, or perhaps a still-life painting, but never a Madonna and Child.

Shirley moved away from the cards to the piles of gay wrapping paper and ribbon that were displayed on a large table. After some thought, she chose several dozen sheets in assorted colours, reds and blacks and golds, with various printed designs upon them. A young girl whom she did not recognise took them from her and rolled them into a cylinder, wrapping them up in a sheet of pale green paper stamped with *Bliss* all over in darker green and securing the end with sellotape, again printed with *Bliss*.

Shirley gave her a five-pound note and waited while the girl, mouthing silently at the till, calculated the change and counted it into her hand.

'Thank you.' Shirley resisted the urge to add 'my dear'. She had done this once to a new young employee and seen her cringe: to some it seemed like patronage. But Bliss's was one of the few places left in England where the reverse applied; no customer, except for an occasional infant in the Stork Bar, was ever addressed as 'dear' or 'love'. One of the earliest and cardinal rules of the staff training programme was that 'madam' and 'sir' prevailed.

The roll of paper tucked like a guardsman's cane under her arm, Shirley walked up the ramp and the short flight of stairs to the ground floor. At once a heady smell from the perfumery department greeted her, the blend of scents that was an infallible titillation to Bertram. A few of the salesgirls noticed her passing, and nudged each other. They smiled self-consciously, and the more poised among them said, 'Good morning, Mrs. Bliss.' Shirley stopped to admire some elaborately packaged bottles, then feared she might be accused of aping the Queen on a royal progress and hurried on. Mildred Smith, now well established among hair ornaments and eye make-up, and wearing a good selection of her wares, peered at her through false eyelashes and thought how awful it must be to be so old. What good could eye-shadow and eye-liner do for such a face? It looked as if Mrs. Bliss thought the position hopeless herself; she seemed innocent of artificial aids, beyond lipstick that was much too dark and thereby gave away her age, since youth favoured pale bloodless pinks verging on anaemia. So much for Shirley's unceasing efforts with moisture cream and covering fluid; Mildred would have been surprised if she could have seen the array of bottles and jars which Shirley used each day.

It was impossible for Shirley to visit the store without walking through every department. Now she took the lift to the first floor, where reigning over Fashions she would find her friend Eileen Westcott. These days, they rarely met, for old Mrs. Westcott took up most of Eileen's time apart from working hours. In their encounters Shirley was able to catch up on the internal politics of the store; Bertram talked to her about general developments and his largest plans, but he did not give her the detailed gossip, which she loved to hear.

Word had got round already that she was in the store, and Eileen was watching for her.

'I've got the kettle on. Come into my office,' she greeted Shirley the moment she appeared through the archway. 'We heard you were in.'

Shirley followed Eileen past the fitting rooms with their curtained doorways into the small office where she dealt with buyers, post orders and stock requirements. On most days Eileen went upstairs to the cafeteria like everybody else for her mid-morning break; but sometimes she was too busy to spare the time, or thought she was, or wilted overmuch, and for these occasions she kept here the means for revival.

Once out of sight of the younger staff, Shirley wrenched off her hat. Down came wisps of her greying hair; she twisted it up impatiently and said:

'It's nice to see you, Eileen. You look tired. How's your mother?'

'Oh, much the same. It's ages since you've been in.' Eileen's voice held, to Shirley's guilty ears, reproach.

'I know.' She did not explain. Bertram did not like her to come in often; he seemed to think her inquisitive if she arrived without a reason; mere interest would not do. 'I've been buying wrapping paper.' She indicated her roll, now dumped on a corner of Eileen's desk.

'They've some pretty things down there on the mezzanine,' said Eileen. She poured boiling water from the kettle into two cups where Nescafé lurked, waiting for transformation, added powdered milk from a tin, and, without asking, sugar. Shirley accepted her cup and sat back in the chair where representatives from fashion wholesalers were wont to seat themselves, hoping to sell Eileen their latest models.

'Tell me all the news.'

Nothing loath, Eileen embarked on the latest instalment of local events. She described first her mother's more trying caprices of the last weeks. The old lady was very forgetful now, and sometimes tyrannical. When this topic was exhausted she moved on to a description of events within the store. Young Paul Jessamy seemed to be making his presence ever more firmly felt at management meetings, she said. Both she and Shirley could remember him as a spotty schoolboy arriving to work as a packer in his school holidays. His parents ran a hotel at Birdsea, and he hated the kitchen tasks there that they thought suitable vacation employment for him. From the first, he loved the store; he had been through several departments, spent a summer in Denmark and a few months in London gaining wider experience, and was now all set to rise high.

'He'll probably take over from Bertie one day,' said Shirley, swinging a loose shoe on the toe of her small, plump foot. She was vain about her feet and often unconsciously drew attention to them in this way.

'He needs to have a bit more spunk,' said Eileen. 'He still moons about after Sally Manners in the most spineless way, whenever she's in sight.'

'It would be quite exciting if she and Paul got married,' Shirley said. 'Almost in the family, you might say.' She went off into a trance and saw Sally floating down the aisle in a mist of tulle, Paul debonair in morning coat, herself shedding quiet tears in the background, and Bertram beaming, dispensing bonhomie, quite forgetting that Sally had a perfectly good father of her own, and unaware

43

that Bertram's emotions on such an occasion would not be truly paternal.

'Well, stranger things have happened.' Eileen set her mouth. 'Not that I'm saying anything against Paul, mind you. He's a good boy and he'd probably train up well to be chairman in time.'

'We'd have to go public first, I suppose,' said Shirley. The company was still a private one, in which she held the greater number of shares. 'Still, don't let's think about such gloomy things now, Eileen. What else has been happening?'

'Well,' Eileen considered. 'Let me see. Oh yes, that nice Marjorie Betts has moved to Lighting and seems much happier. We had tea together yesterday and she was full of it. She thinks the world of Bertram.' Here, out of hearing of the other staff, Eileen used his name as she had for years since they were all young in the days of Hawkins' Hardware, long before he became the ruler of Bliss's.

Shirley glowed at praise of Bertie.

'I should think it's much better for her than Toiletries,' she said. 'I shouldn't enjoy that department. It's draughty by the door, and all these new trends in make-up take a lot of keeping up with.'

'Indeed they do,' said Eileen. 'You could spend a fortune on your face. Most of these youngsters seem to.'

'There was a new little thing selling eye make-up, I noticed,' Shirley said.

'Oh, that would be Mildred Smith. She's the one who was swopped with Marjorie,' said Eileen. 'It's much more suitable this way round.'

'Well, personally I like to buy cream and stuff from somebody nearer my own age,' Shirley confessed. 'These chits of girls scare me. You feel they're thinking, poor old bag, what's the use of her trying.'

'Well, I daresay we'd look even more hopeless naked as

44

we came,' said Eileen with a chuckle. 'You might as well say the same here, in Fashions.'

'Oh no,' Shirley protested. 'Young things can wear almost anything and look nice. We oldies need to pay a bit more and take some trouble.'

'I must say, I rather like to see the kids going home in their little skirts and tights,' Eileen said. 'They look so gay. Mr. Thomas finds all that leg very shocking. He's no end of a prude.'

'Well, what do you expect after years of life with only a parrot?' said Shirley.

'Even he must have been young once,' Eileen pointed out. 'Though he's looked just the same for as long as I can remember. Shirley, where are you going for lunch? Shall we go to the Copper Kettle?'

Occasionally they did this, eating steak-and-kidney pie or roast lamb in a café down the street much frequented by the store's country customers.

'Oh, I can't! I'm meeting Bertie at The Star.' Shirley knew that it was a rare treat for Eileen to escape and have other company than that of her mother or her colleagues; most days she lunched in respected solitude, or with Mr. Thomas, in a corner of the cafeteria reserved by custom for the senior staff. 'But look, I'll come in again next week,' she decided. 'We'll meet then for lunch. How about Tuesday?'

'Oh, lovely. That will be something to look forward to,' said Eileen. 'Well, I suppose I'd better go and see what the girls are up to,' she added, and had just risen to her feet when the office door opened and Joan Seabright came in, looking grave.

'Good morning, Mrs. Bliss,' said Joan. She was smartly dressed in a charcoal jersey suit with a triangle of shocking pink blouse visible at the neck.

Shirley felt a little like a schoolboy truant caught by his

teacher at being thus discovered, gossiping with the staff, by her husband's secretary.

But greater events than the detection of Shirley hob-nobbing with the rank and file weighed upon Mrs. Seabright.

'Miss Westcott, I'm afraid I have bad news for you,' she said. 'Mr. Bliss asked me to come and tell you personally. Your mother has been taken ill. A neighbour found her lying unconscious on the floor.'

'Oh no!' Eileen's face lost even the little colour it had.

'They think it was a stroke. She's been taken to hospital,' said Joan Seabright.

Shirley had risen and collected her bag, parcel and hat during this exchange.

'You must go at once. I'll take you there,' she said.

'Is there anything I can do?' Joan asked. 'How lucky you're here, Mrs. Bliss.'

'Yes.' Shirley was almost brusque with the urgency of suddenly having a cause for action. 'Will you tell my husband I'm going with Miss Westcott and won't be able to meet him? She ignored Eileen's faint protests, merely saying, 'Of course I'm staying with you, Eileen, don't be silly.'

'Just leave it to me,' said Joan Seabright. 'Can I do anything else?' She glanced round the office, which apart from the tea-cups just used was orderly.

'I don't think so, thank you.' Eileen looked distractedly about. 'I'll just go and tell Maud,' she said, and went into the department where her minions were attending to the wants of various customers.

Shirley followed her out, and waited while she fetched her coat and scarf. Soon they were both in her little car, weaving in and out of the busy traffic towards the gaunt Victorian building which was the General Hospital.

'I should never have left her alone,' Eileen was lamenting. 'This wouldn't have happened if I'd been at home.'

'Nonsense, Eileen. For one thing, you don't know exactly what has happened,' said Shirley robustly. 'And, for another, you couldn't possibly be with her every minute of the day. It might have happened if you simply went to post a letter.' Besides, they had to live. 'Anyway,' she added, 'it may not be as bad as you think.'

But it was bad. Old Mrs. Westcott was certainly dying, although she might take some few days to accomplish it. She lay, frail and already wax-like, under blankets, screened off in a side ward, breathing noisily.

Eileen and Shirley sat together beside the high bed, waiting. No one could do anything but wait. A doctor spoke to them, explaining. Sister came and went. Nurses looked in and out, felt the old lady's pulse, and withdrew.

Eileen suddenly came out of the stupor she seemed to be in.

'Oh, goodness, Shirley, I've just remembered that the traveller from Madame Models is coming in at four. They're a new house, you know, catering for older women.'

'Well, Maud can manage, can't she?' Shirley asked. 'She's a capable girl.' Maud Wilson was Eileen's under-buyer.

'Yes, she is. If it was anything else I wouldn't worry, but this is rather special. Maud is used to younger styles. I attend to all the buying for the older customers.'

This was true.

'Couldn't Maud put him off? You could see him next week.'

'I want to get the orders through before Christmas. That might not give enough time. And he'll be on his way by now.'

'Would it help if I went back and lent a hand?' Shirley considered Eileen was unnecessarily anxious, but it was typical. 'Maybe I can do more for you there than here.' She looked at the form on the bed. 'At least I know some-

47

thing about clothes for older women. Maud and I should manage between us.'

'Oh, bless you, Shirley. Would you?'

'I'll get over there right away. Just tell me what you want done,' said Shirley. 'I'll come back here when we close, and you're spending the night with us. No argument.'

Some time later Bertram was walking through the fashion department in the store; in the distance he saw a figure wearing the dark green jersey dress that was uniform for the senior salesladies. He stopped, for once astounded, as he recognised his wife. At that moment Shirley disappeared, leading a customer to the fitting-rooms, and Maud Wilson swam with her flat-footed walk up to him across the thick grey carpet that covered the floor. Normally she maintained an expression of mask-like inscrutability which she considered appropriate to her lofty position, but now she beamed with undisguised delight.

'Oh, Mr. Bliss, your wife is wonderful!' she exclaimed in her nasal, Midland accent. 'She's taken over a hundred pounds already this afternoon. She came to help me with the representative from Madame Models, and she's getting her eye in first, she says.'

Bertram was, for once, speechless. He looked at Miss Wilson and then across at the curtains through which Shirley had vanished.

'We'll manage splendidly, Mr. Bliss. Don't worry,' Maud assured him.

'I have no doubt you will,' he said, slowly. 'Yes, between the pair of you, I'm sure you will.'

He did not linger to speak to Shirley when she finished with her customer. Instead, he walked away and returned to his office, where he immediately rang for his secretary.

When Joan Seabright appeared he wasted no time.

48

'Joan, did you know Mrs. Bliss had stepped into Miss Westcott's shoes this afternoon?' he asked.

Now it was Joan's turn to appear at a loss. She had made an earlier expedition herself to ascertain whether a crisis had developed. None should, for delegation was the golden rule throughout the store. She had seen a flushed, triumphant Shirley, wedged into a dress from her own department that was a trifle tight across the bust, for her own tan suit made her look, she said, like a customer, busy completing a sales slip in Miss Westcott's book. At first amazed, Joan had quickly sensed the delight of the young assistants who were near; far from resenting what in someone of another character might have looked like interference, they were grateful. Joan noticed their youthfulness; only Maud was over twenty : they needed someone older in the background, and Shirley, though a rare visitor, had always been popular with the staff.

'We're taking the customers in turns,' Shirley told Joan. 'That's only fair. We don't want Eileen to lose on the day. Please don't tell my husband, Mrs. Seabright.' Here she blushed slightly. 'He might think I couldn't manage. Give me time to prove I can still do a job of work, even for just a few hours.'

So Joan agreed.

Now she told Bertram : 'Mrs. Bliss has been marvellous. The girls were very glad to have her with them. Some of the older customers can be very trying.'

'I know.'

Miss Westcott had her special customers, elderly ladies, many from the country villages around, whom she had looked after for years, whose ways and tastes she understood; they would not trust the girls : it was their youth the older customers feared.

'It's only for today, of course,' he said.

6

But it was not only for a day. Old Mrs. Westcott lingered on, blessedly oblivious herself, but to the agony of her watching daughter, for more than forty-eight hours. After the brief, bleak service in which her physical remains were disposed of at the local crematorium, Eileen collapsed. During this time Shirley had spent at least five hours a day doing what she called 'keeping an eye on things' in the fashion department. Now she became still more active. Eileen was put to bed in the spare room at Cedar Grange, cosseted, plied with tempting trays of invalid fare and given books to read while Shirley continued to make daily forays into the store. In a week she lost seven pounds in weight and gained immeasurable confidence and vitality. Before, the days had been too full of hours; now there were not enough.

On the Sunday, Eileen came down to lunch, her first appearance since her arrival. She picked at the roast chicken and sprouts on her plate, then retreated again, wan, to her bed. Bertram arranged himself at his desk near the window with his stamps and began to examine them; Shirley, really tired, put up her feet on the sofa and pretended to read *The Sunday Express*. Before long she was gently snoozing, and woke to hear Bertram's voice.

'This can't go on,' he declared. 'There's no need for you to do Eileen's job, Shirley. I'm surprised the girls haven't objected. They may think it shows lack of confidence in them. Maud Wilson is perfectly competent to take over.'

'I know she is, but they're very busy just now, and I only go in for a few hours,' said Shirley. 'Eileen likes to know what's happening. It keeps her from fretting. Besides, I enjoy it.'

'Hm.' Bertie frowned. It was true that there had not been a single word of complaint, rather the reverse, for Joan Seabright was not alone in her admiration for Shirley's efforts; but his sense of the fitness of things was affronted.

'Eileen will soon be better,' Shirley said. 'But she ought to go away for a break before she starts work again. Couldn't we send her off for a week or two, Bertie? Somewhere warm? A cruise, perhaps. She's had an awful time these last few years and no proper holiday for ages. The strain was much worse than anyone realised.'

This was a just verdict, and an echo of what the doctor had said.

'You should go with her,' said Bertram, inspired.

'Oh no, not without you.' Shirley at once shut her mind to the intoxicating but unlikely vision she immediately had of herself and Eileen riding camels to see the Sphinx. Better, far, and clearly her duty, to stay here and keep Eileen's place at Bliss's warm for her. A niggling fear that her friend might never take control again lurked in her mind: Maud could supplant her. But this would be prevented if Shirley were there.

'We'll see,' Bertie said. 'I don't want you working in the store, Shirley. It's not what's expected of the chairman's wife.'

'I worked in the shop before you did,' said Shirley with spirit.

'Things were very different then,' Bertram reminded her, in a patient tone.

'I'm staying till Eileen comes back,' Shirley said stubbornly. 'I enjoy it, Bertie. I'm bored here all day on my own. It isn't as if we'd a family to keep me busy.'

'That's not exactly a new situation, my dear,' said Bertram. He picked up a stamp in his tweezers and scrutinised it intently through a magnifying glass.

'I'm still the majority shareholder. You can't stop me

if I insist,' said Shirley. It was the first time she had ever thus defied him, and the first time she had reminded him of the original source of their prosperity.

Bertram chose to be grieved rather than angry at this want of taste.

'Please consider what you are saying, my dear,' he said. 'Without my judgement and foresight you might very well still be behind the counter in an ironmonger's. That's a very different matter from playing at shops for a few hours a day in Bliss's.'

'I did it for years when I was young. It didn't hurt me then, and it wouldn't hurt me now!' cried Shirley. 'In any case, don't you be so sure that all the credit's yours. Who thought of opening the babywear department in the beginning? Tell me that!' A surge of rebellious energy sent the colour into her face. She sat forward on the edge of the sofa, her knees together, her heavy bosom projected aggressively.

'Calm yourself.' Bertram would not yield to emotion; he prided himself on supreme powers of self-control no matter what the provocation. As a taunted child, his anger had always turned inwards, spurring him to efforts to excel. Shirley must be subdued; such a revolt could not be tolerated. She must be forced to leave the store and settle down again. Clearly the quickest way to get Shirley out of the fashion department was to speed Eileen back to it; the best method might well be to despatch her on a restorative holiday. At least the cruise was Shirley's idea.

'Your suggestion of a holiday for Eileen is worth exploring,' he conceded. 'I'll telephone Dr. Simpson and see when he thinks she could go.'

The prospect of the cruise had a magical effect upon Eileen. She was overcome by Bertram's generosity when he announced that he would pay for it, and begged Shirley to go with her, but when forced to accept that this could not be, she produced a widowed friend from her youth who had had a spectacular Premium Bond win and longed to blow some of the proceeds on a glorious burst of foreign travel.

On a Saturday morning in November, Eileen was to depart. Shirley insisted on going with her to London, to see that she safely met Violet Pringle as arranged, and caught the right train for Southampton. They left Sedgemouth on the early express, after travelling to the station in a taxi. Bertram was to follow, later in the day; theatre tickets had been booked for himself and Shirley; they would spend the night in town and return home on Sunday, a jaunt which he hoped would remind Shirley of her good fortune and where her duty lay.

Both women were quite excited as, with some ado, they were stowed into the train by the only visible porter.

'Oh, I envy you today,' said Shirley, looking out of the window at the dark, wintry day. 'Imagine it, soon you'll be basking in the sun.'

'I wish you were coming too,' said Eileen.

'So do I, but I wouldn't enjoy it without Bertie,' said Shirley. Having uttered the words, she suddenly wondered if they were true.

'I suppose you wouldn't.' Eileen believed it, anyway.

'Mind you send a card from every port,' Shirley commanded.

During the past week her pace had quickened; she had acquired a waistline, and a new alertness; it was she who had suggested that Bertram should come to London too, and he had agreed because there was a trade exhibition on where he might profitably spend a few hours in the afternoon. He had turned round the whole scheme and made it sound as though it had been all his own idea.

The journey soon passed. When the train drew in to Paddington, Shirley took charge, found a porter, and in no time at all they were in a taxi bowling along towards

Waterloo. They were to meet Violet by the News Cinema, and she was already there, waiting for them, when they arrived, a beaming smile on her pink, round face under a woolly purple hat, and zippered bags and cases stacked around her. She was as excited as a child, hugging Eileen against her ancient musquash coat and barely managing to utter a few grave words of consolation before bubbling into a chatter of anticipation. Shirley realised that a middle-aged widow who lived on a pension and yet would happily blue a large part of a financial windfall on one brief spree must have a carefree disposition; foolhardy, some might say, but Shirley applauded the gesture. This little woman would live on the memory of her experience for years; she would cheer Eileen up; you could not be dismal for long in her company. The three were soon giggling merrily in the station restaurant over double gins and tonics and the good hot lunch that was intended to fortify the travellers until they embarked.

Shirley stood on the platform and waved them out of sight as the boat train bore them away. She felt deflated. Slowly she walked back through the barrier, and collected her own small case from the left luggage where she had deposited it while she saw the others off. Outside the station, the day was grey and a fine rain was falling; it was just the weather to leave England. She wondered how to spend the afternoon. As it was Saturday, the shops would be shut. She decided to go to the hotel and get rid of her suitcase, then, unenthusiastically, that she should seize this chance to improve her mind by a cultural visit to some museum or picture gallery.

The hotel room was utterly impersonal but comfortable. The twin beds were covered in coffee-coloured candlewick, the dressing-table was made of silvered wood, there were pale rayon curtains, and a microscopic bathroom was attached. Shirley unpacked the black velvet cocktail dress she intended to wear in the evening and hung it in the cupboard; she had lost so much weight in the past few weeks that it needed taking in. Next, she washed her face, pondered, and felt sad. In her mind she followed Eileen and Violet; by now they were probably chatting with their fellow travellers as they rode onwards in the train. Perhaps she had been stupid in refusing to go; after all, Bertram had favoured the idea, but would she have enjoyed it without him? A vague impression of moonlight and phosphorescent water came into her mind; she stood, in imagination, leaning upon the ship's rail, a shadowy male figure at her side : was it Bertie? No, it was taller and broader altogether. Two heads leaned close together; a hand caressed hers; a face rather like Gregory Peck's turned towards her.

At this point Shirley's mental movie switched off. She tried to make it operate again, replacing Gregory Peck firmly with an image of Bertram, but the thrill was absent. It was no good; facts must be faced and the truth was that since Bliss's had grown so large and so successful, he had drawn away from her, excluding her more and more from what went on at the store and trying to keep her partitioned off in a domestic box occupying just a small section of his time. If only they had had a son, everything would have been so different; they would have remained united in the endeavour to build up his future. This old wound still hurt. Unconsciously, she ran her hands over her hips and stomach, and two tears slid down her cheeks as a wave of self-pity hit her.

'It's all that gin,' she told herself crossly. Drinking at midday was always unwise. She blew her nose, washed her face again, and made it up anew, powdering it thickly; emotion and alcohol combined to make her more flushed than usual. With grim concentration she forced her feet back into her smart patent shoes, put on her mink coat, picked up her bag, gloves and umbrella, and made for the door. Action was essential, or she would end up wallowing

55

in woe, and be a poor spectacle indeed when Bertie arrived.

The porter called a taxi for her. As she pressed a shilling into his hand she wondered where to go. In desperation, she decided.

'The British Museum,' she cried, climbing in. She would discover what the Elgin Marbles were, a matter about which she was completely ignorant.

Meanwhile, back in Sedgemouth on that Saturday morning, Bertram finished his breakfast in peaceful solitude after Eileen and Shirley had gone. He drove slowly into town, enjoying the contrast between the raw, dank day outside and the upholstered comfort of his pleasantly heated car. This life was indeed a far cry from that of little Bertram Bliss who had played hopscotch in the street with the milkman's son while *The Merry Peasant* came echoing from the front room of his mother's house as her latest pupil struggled with the piano. Barely a day passed when he did not reflect briefly on these lines.

Joan Seabright did not come in on Saturdays. A girl from the main office dealt with any urgent correspondence that could not wait until after the weekend, but this morning there was nothing of such importance. Bertram walked round his office, studying the paintings on the wall, then peered out of the window across the street at the property he coveted. It would cost a packet, if he could ever get hold of it, but the bank would back such a venture. All the household departments, under the rule of Paul Jessamy, could be transferred and expanded. He dreamed about this for a while. Shirley had suggested opening a branch in another town as a means of growth, but Bertram did not want his empire to be so widely spread. Though he preached delegation, he still felt it would be difficult to keep on top of two establishments divided by twenty or more miles; a powerful manager would have to reign in one of them. If he could have put a son in it

56

would have been different. He thought about the family he had once expected to beget. Never in all the years of their marriage had he reproached Shirley with her failure to conceive, he congratulated himself. He was sad about it, but resigned and silent. His noble conduct made him throw out his chest proudly whenever he thought of it.

At half past nine he pressed the buzzer on his desk and asked for Sally to attend upon him. Uninterrupted, they could discuss the Christmas windows. The Three Kings, now many times multiplied, were stacked ready to appear next week. Father Christmas had been re-engaged and would be waiting at the end of a mystery camel ride along canvas passages in Toyland; the Yule season need be held back no longer. While Bertram waited for Sally to appear he planned to summon coffee for them both, thus legitimately detaining her for at least half an hour. Dare he invite her to lunch? No: prudence forbade; he must be as Caesar's wife. But he would draw her out in conversation and ask about her life. She must have problems he could help to solve. She often looked pale and tired; he would persuade her to confide in him. He dwelt fondly on this scheme, and had reached a point where she began to sob, so that he must proffer a spotless handkerchief and an avuncular encircling arm, when there came a tap at the door.

To his eager summons entered not Sally, but Wendy. Bertram was taken aback, but, bland as ever, hid it.

'Sally and I changed weekends, Mr. Bliss,' said Wendy. 'She's off today.'

Bertram frowned. He looked crossly at Wendy as she stood in the doorway, her eyes almost obscured by her straggly fringe. He did not like surprises of this sort; however, he made a swift mental adjustment and observed that in her leggy, youthful way she was pretty and appealing.

'Well, come along in, Wendy,' he said, beginning to

57

smile. 'I'm sure you can tell me all I want to know.' He got up from his chair and emerged from behind his desk to urge her forward, a hand upon her arm; it felt thin under her nylon overall. A waft of Coty's L'Aimant reached his nose as she moved, and his nostrils widened.

'Sit down, my dear,' he said. 'I'll have some coffee sent to us; it's a cold day and I'm sure you'd enjoy a cup. You young women never eat sufficient breakfast, that I know.'

He retreated again to his own side of the desk and sat down in his swivel executive chair.

Wendy could not very well refuse. She began to store up the details of all this to relate to Sally on Monday: how the old boy's face had fallen when she appeared, not Sally; and how he had decided to cut his losses and make do. She knew he would attempt no more than the touch on her arm already made. Bertram's pleasures were over-sublimated. She crossed her legs and waited; she knew that he would only talk.

7

Bertram's mood was gay and carefree as he drove the Rover out of the yard and edged into the busy street. A passing Ford Anglia paused respectfully to admit him into the stream of traffic that flowed past the rear entrance of the store; he gestured gracious acknowledgement with a wave of his tweed arm as he rolled the car forward to merge with the tide. He had, during the morning, done just enough work to justify his refusal on the plea of pressure to accompany Shirley and Eileen on the early train, so that now, as he changed gear and moved on towards the centre of the town, he basked in a glow of virtue. The traffic lights turned to red as he approached, and he eased the clutch, sitting there relaxed, small and observant, peering out while a surge of pedestrians crossed the road, brushing against his radiator grille. He knew many of Sedgemouth's citizens by sight, if not by name, and they knew him; his sleek car and his compact figure were familiar in the streets. A woman recognised him now, nodded and smiled tentatively, too heavily burdened by shopping bags and bundles to do more. It was Marjorie Betts, from Lighting. Bertram leaned across and swiftly wound down the nearside window of the car, calling to her. She scuttled at once to his side, and heard him offer her a lift.

'Oh, how kind. Thank you, Mr. Bliss,' she gasped.

The traffic lights changed to green, but Bertram was unruffled by the delay caused while she climbed in, dumping her packages around her feet; he paid no heed to the hooting cars behind.

'You live in The Grove, don't you?' he asked, as they finally moved off.

How did he remember such details? Marjorie, who worked alternate Saturdays under the current shift system obtaining at the store, had still to buy Wellington boots for Michael, but she abandoned the project for today; Monday's lunch hour would give her time for that, and he would have to manage over the weekend in his too small, leaky old pair.

'Yes, I do,' she said aloud. 'Isn't it taking you out of your way?' Everyone knew that the chairman lived on Castle Hill in a fortress of great luxury.

'Not at all. I'm going to the station and it's no further to go by way of The Grove. I've plenty of time before the London train leaves.' Mr. Bliss was expansive.

She sat back, protesting no more, thankful to rest against the comfortable leather upholstery and breathe the warm air circulated so efficient'y throughout the car

59

instead of the dank November chill. Protected from the bustling multitude, she was carried homewards. How kind was Mr. Bliss. Cautiously she glanced sideways at him : his countenance exuded goodwill; benevolence was reflected through his spectacles. His hands, in expensive leather gloves, made the minimal movements as he guided the car competently through the heavy weekend traffic.

As if he caught the drift of her thoughts, Bertram spoke. 'Do you drive, Mrs. Betts?'

'Not now. I used to,' she replied. She used to do a lot of things that were now far removed from her daily experience.

'You should keep it up,' said Bertram mildly. Her Saturday shopping would be easier if she could use the family car. He assumed there was one, however lowly.

'I'd be nervous in all this traffic. It gets worse and worse,' she said. 'And there's never anywhere to park. Besides, my husband has a company car and I may not use it.'

'Oh. Too bad.' Bertram negotiated a narrow chasm between a bus and a pantechnicon. 'What does your husband do?' He ought to know the answer to this; he'd meant to look it up in the personnel files.

'He travels in dry goods,' said Marjorie flatly, not adding, but only for the moment, till he gets sacked again for being drunk and slanging a customer.

It sounded banal; Bertram pictured a jolly, red-faced grocer, lentils in a packet, then dismissed the image. Someone or something must be the cause of Marjorie's constant look of strain. He docketed a mental memo : investigate Betts.

Too soon for Marjorie, they turned into The Grove.

'Please drop me here. I can easily walk now,' she said as they swept round the corner. But Bertram drove steadily on.

'Which is your house?' he asked, and was perforce

guided to Number 65, a semi-detached villa with rendered façade, and timbered elevations that had once been painted black and now were peeling. Straggly dark cupressus trees, dripping with wet, formed a barricade between it and Number 63 next door. A rickety fence further divided them. Marjorie struggled to extricate herself and her possessions as the car halted outside this dwelling, which looked utterly dismal in the grey wintry day.

'I'd ask you in, Mr. Bliss,' she began anxiously, 'but . . .'

Before she could devise a valid excuse, Bertram intervened.

'My train won't wait, I'm afraid. Another time, Mrs. Betts.'

'Yes, of course. I hope you won't be late. Thank you so much for bringing me home.'

'A pleasure.'

She stood to watch him go. He drove to the end of the road and turned off, lost to sight, in a direction which would bring him to the rear approach to the station. He had, in fact, travelled some distance out of his way to help her. When he had quite vanished, Marjorie picked up her baskets from the pavement, squared her shoulders, and let herself in through the garden gate which sagged from its hinges and needed a coat of paint. She was home early, thanks to her benefactor, so that precious time had been saved, but she must face the sooner whatever Peter had dreamed up as a method of torment this weekend.

Bertram, alone, continued blithely on his way. He liked smoothing people's paths, and the sense of power such actions yielded. He meditated now in a complacent manner about the additional half-hour or more that Mrs. Betts might enjoy in the bosom of her family. Whatever the grocer might be like, the children at least would gain from his Boy Scout deed. A pleasant woman, Mrs. Betts, if a little mousy; she must have been pretty once.

There was no question about Bertram's preference for

travelling to London by train rather than by car; immured in a first-class compartment, he could study his papers and sort out business problems in comparative peace. To drive up, especially on so murky a day, would be no pleasure. He bought his return ticket, paid his parking fee, and stepped on to the platform three minutes before the train was due : perfect timing, no waste. By such means, employing every minute of his day, he made subtle gains in each activity of his life. To sit at home reading a book merely for pleasure was to him a profligate act; the only leisure activity he really indulged was philately, and even then he was always alive to the possibility of selling and buying stamps to advantage. It was not mere relaxation; it was also lucrative. Today's journey would be spent studying literature about the trade exhibition he would visit this afternoon. He remained quite still as the train came in, for he knew that the first-class compartments would halt directly opposite where he waited; there he stood, a neat, unostentatious figure, soberly clad in an expensive black overcoat, with dark worsted legs appearing below that ended in shiny, elastic-sided shoes, for he was, though middle-aged, a modern man.

The journey passed swiftly, profitably spent. At Paddington he took a taxi to the exhibition, and after he had seen all that interested him, he proceeded to the hotel, where by now Shirley would be waiting. He knew that she would be stretched out on her bed, resting, wrapped in her peach dressing-gown but otherwise naked and possibly expectant of overtures from him. Of course, she would first want to unburden herself of the tale of Eileen's departure and he must be ready to listen patiently to her words. It was a pity she had not agreed to go too; he was gratified, naturally, that she preferred to stay with him, but of course it was only to be expected. However, he wanted her out of the store, where her presence was a constant embarrassment to him. Her rebellious remarks of a short while before had alarmed him; he wanted no repetition. She owed her financial security entirely to his prescience; time had blunted ardour between them, but there was little discord : so long as he was there, she was content, but without his guidance he was sure she would be like a ship without a helm. He it was who had steered her towards the Townswomen's Guild and the Society for Floral Art, suitable occupations for a woman in her circumstances, and especially so since she could not acquire influential friends through the bond of growing children : means had to be found for social advancement, and Bertram had pointed the way. His ambition was not merely material; already the friend of the Mayor, most of the councillors of Sedgemouth and the acknowledged leader of the tradesmen, Bertram sought still greater glory; his cause would be damaged if the wives of men he aimed to meet as equals found Shirley selling them dresses.

She was not at the hotel.

She had signed in, but the key was at the desk. Put out, Bertram ascended to their room. There was her dressing-gown, indeed, spread across the bed, but empty; her feathered mules were neatly side by side upon the floor. He unpacked his own tomato-coloured pyjamas, ivory-backed brushes and dark green silk dressing-gown. Then he ran a bath. When she arrived, she would have to wait if she wanted one; she would have to wait, too, for anything else she might be anticipating. Bertram took off his tie as the water ran, filling the tiny bathroom with steam which spread into the bedroom. She would simply have to go on waiting.

Shirley had, with some trouble, found the Elgin Marbles. Gold and silver chalices of great splendour had sidetracked her on the way; she gazed, entranced, at treasures of such richness and historical import that her imagination boggled in an attempt to understand what she saw. Finally, she moved on, hired a recorded guide, and with this plugged into her ear walked hypnotically round the frieze studying it diligently. Sated at last with Grecian legend, she wandered out among cases of ancient manuscripts and shelves of leather-bound books, still somewhat bemused.

By now, Bertie would be just about leaving his exhibition, she supposed. She started to look forward to their evening; they seldom came to London. Their sole excursions into pleasure-seeking were occasional dinners out with Bertram's business friends and their wives. Shirley began to think more tenderly of him, and regretted the twin beds in their hotel: after the stimulus of an evening at the theatre and an expensive meal, who knew what might result? She sighed, aware from experience that anticipation often led to anticlimax.

A flurry of rain caught her as she walked out of the Museum, down the steps and into the street, chilling her sturdy legs in their non-run fifteen denier. She looked in vain up and down the road for a taxi: since none was in sight, she walked on, her umbrella up, feeling the droplets of water from the pavement splashing her calves. Ahead, the light of a cruising taxi showed at last and she made ready to hail it, but it stopped for someone else before reaching her. She walked a further hundred yards before another came and saw her signalling. Thankfully she clambered in. At least in here she was protected from the wet. Her feet ached, and she began to regret her expedition; she was tired and might not look her best for Bertie. As the taxi moved on, she caught sight of a clock on a building outside, and saw with a shock that it was much later than she had thought. She looked at her watch, and then held it against her ear. It had stopped. She sat forward anxiously on the taxi seat as if to spur it on to carry her the faster. Thus it was that, while stationary in a traffic-block, she noticed a couple on the kerb, collars up against the rain, the girl with a scarf over her head. They were linked, arm-in-arm, faces turned intently to each other, unaware of anyone else, and as the taxi moved forward Shirley saw that the girl was Sally Manners.

She did not recognise the man.

8

When Paul Jessamy left the store on Saturday evening his spirits were low. It had been a hard day; Saturdays were always busy. However, eventually half past five came; the doors were locked, the lights were dimmed, the final straggling customers were shepherded civilly out-side, and everyone went home. Paul was one of the last to leave; he and Mr. Thomas were responsible this month for locking up and handing over to the night-watchmen. The senior male staff took this duty in turn, and it was a rare night when Mr. Bliss himself left before the last patrol was made to make sure that no one was locked in. Paul thought it would be simple for a determined thief, vandal or vagrant to hide in a cupboard or under a dustsheet, and wait until all was quiet before emerging to wreak his mischief, but it had never happened yet. Because of this obsession, he poked about and prodded shrouded racks of garments in the expectation of disclosing a lurking villain.

Mr. Thomas longed to be at home with his slippers, his pipe and his parrot. He had varicose veins which ached at the end of the day, and an urge for tobacco which he would not gratify in front of the staff. He smoked in the cafeteria after meals, but never in the passages; an example must be set. An odour of Three Nuns clung to his clothes at all times, though he was unaware of it. Patiently he waited for Paul, thinking of how he would spend Sunday. He would/rise at his usual Sunday time of eight o'clock, an hour later than working days; then he would have an extra cup of tea with his breakfast egg, clean out the parrot's cage, and take the bird, upon his arm, for a stroll around the house, or the garden if it was fine. After that he would walk down to the local for a pint, a chat, and his lunch, as was his weekend custom, then return home to his parrot and a nap on the sofa, punctuated by an occasional glance at *The People*. After tea he would walk to the chapel for evening service, where sometimes he played the harmonium. He might go back to the manse for an hour, or, if it was a fine night, take a short stroll on the common. Then it would be bedtime, and up early again on Monday for another routine week.

Mr. Thomas, apart from his parrot, was quite alone in the world. Long ago, just after the First World War, he had supposed that in time he would share his life with an acquiescent female creature at his side who would cook and clean for him, and perform other functions about which he mused only vaguely; he met various girls at whist drives and church socials, but when it came to the point of enfolding a soft form in an embrace, a vital part of Mr. Thomas shrank away; he could not do it. There was something repellent in yielding flesh and open lips as proffered by Gladys Hughes in the front parlour of her parents' home after a mission meeting. He had no urge to explore any further delights. It was easy to walk away from what was, to him, no temptation. Ladies he met were left in unexplained bewilderment, until finally he was accepted as a confirmed bachelor. He enjoyed the company of Miss Westcott, who even when young was always sensible, and maintained a strong sense of filial duty. As they grew older together in the service of Bliss's, Mr. Thomas often shared his corner table in the cafeteria

66

with her, and sometimes escorted her to the bus-stop whence they both set forth homewards in opposing directions. He visited her mother, too, from time to time, and read the old lady selected passages from his favourite works, the Book of Job, for instance, and *Pilgrim's Progress,* until tactfully, at last, Eileen hinted that her mother had grown too frail to pay attention. Now she was dead, poor old soul, and her daughter left alone, another solitary like himself. She should purchase a pet, a budgerigar, perhaps, and join the local Cage Bird Society of which he himself was a founder member. He would be happy to instruct her in the care and management of any feathered friend, and even aid in its selection.

Paul came at last, content with the security of the store, having had his usual chat with the watchmen while they unpacked their sandwiches and thermos flasks in their headquarters.

He and Mr. Thomas travelled home on the same bus. They walked together to the stop and climbed aboard, Paul standing aside politely to allow Mr. Thomas to mount first, as was his due. There was quite a crowd waiting in the light drizzle that fell this evening, and when the bus halted everyone jostled impatiently, anxious to escape from the chilly damp as soon as possible. A sharp umbrella ferrule jabbed Paul in the calf and he winced.

'Oh, sorry, Mr. Jessamy! I hope I didn't hurt you.'

Hermione Tipps, from the typists' pool, had decided on desperate measures. For weeks she had watched Paul pass the open door of her office as he went about his tasks; he even came in, from time to time, with papers to be typed; but he never spared her a glance. She prowled through Household whenever she dared desert her desk, and made excuses to pursue queries in his little office at the back of the department, but though civil if forced to speak, Paul showed no desire to develop their acquaintance.

'Not at all, Miss Tipps,' he said now, heroically, sure

67

that a large bruise was already appearing on his leg. He stood back to let her precede him into the interior of the bus. There was just one seat left, beside Mr. Thomas. Smiling at Paul, Miss Tipps subsided into it. Her short coat shot upwards, and her sturdy thighs, in white fishnet tights, were left exposed. Mr. Thomas shrank back in disgust from this display of so much nearly naked flesh. He looked away, wrinkling his nose, and contrived to move is own bony haunches even further from the loathsome spectacle. Paul, however, had noticed Hermione's gay smile as she looked up at him. He naturally enjoyed the sight of female legs and it was mere reflex that caused him to glance down at her plump knees. She wore high brown boots, so that most of her was well protected from the weather : a mere isthmus of barely covered limb connected boots to mini-skirt and the regions beyond.

She had large blue eyes, the colour of cornflowers.

At the back of Paul's mind was still the image of Sally. Only yesterday he had asked her to go with him to a symphony concert in the Town Hall in three weeks' time. He was certain she could not be already booked up for that date, but she had said she was. He knew that it was no good to persist, yet he was reluctant to give up hope. He had felt sure that there was more to link them than just enjoyment of the moment during the months when she had helped him sail his boat and gone swimming with him. But last April she had gone on holiday to Greece and had returned altered, remote and unapproachable. Since then she had refused all his invitations and resisted every effort he had made to prolong contact.

The bus reached The Grove. Paul said goodbye to Mr. Thomas, who must travel on for another mile, and nodded at Hermione, but saw that she was getting off too. Did she live this way? He had never seen her on the bus before. He was a well-mannered young man, and he turned to help her after he had reached the kerb himself. Hermione

68

eagerly took his extended hand and jumped down beside him. She was small, much smaller than Sally; her head, with the long blonde hair now covered by a scarlet scarf, reached only to his shoulder.

He said: 'Do you live in The Grove too?'

'No, up the other way.' Hermione gestured in the direction taken by the departing bus. In fact, she lived two stops on, but had decided to stake all tonight on a gamble. She had loitered about until she saw Paul emerge from the staff door at the store, and then followed at a distance, unobserved among the throng, determined to attract his notice somehow. When he got off the bus she made ready to pursue. She would impress herself upon him so that on Monday, when they met, as meet they would, he must perforce acknowledge her.

She was very young. Her cheeks were round and the whites of her eyes were so clear that they looked almost blue.

Paul said suddenly: 'I suppose you're already going out tonight? You wouldn't be free to have a meal and perhaps go to the cinema?'

Hermione battled with herself. A girl should retain some pride. But if she refused he might never invite her again. It was a short fight, and ended in compromise with only half a lie.

'I was going out, but my friend's got a cold.'

It was true that Deidre, who was her confidante, had a cold; they usually went to the pictures together on Saturday nights if nothing better offered, but they had a pact to release one another at a moment's notice if some dishy fellow hove on either's horizon. Hermione willed Paul to assume that her unidentified friend was male.

'You can? Oh, good. I'll pick you up in about an hour, then.'

Paul ran a small, old sports car, but seldom travelled

69

in it to work because of the parking problem. The bus was as quick.

'No, I'll meet you somewhere, that would be best,' said Hermione mysteriously.

'Are you sure?' He looked surprised. Perhaps her father resented young men calling for her. 'Well, shall we make it seven o'clock in The Bell? It's handy, and we can have a drink and decide what to do.'

'Fine. See you, then.'

'Yes.'

Transformed within, Hermione was wafted on her way up the road. The wind blew round her thighs, and the rain slid down her coat, but her heart beat fast : it had worked. Boldness was all.

Paul, too, walked off with less leaden steps than had been his recent wont. Someone, at least, seemed pleased to be invited out by him. If Sally despised him, it did not mean that all girls would. He thought fleetingly of Mr. Thomas, and pictured him still sitting in the bus, narrow, shrivelled, huddled in his corner. He had not appeared to recognise Hermione, yet he must have done so, for his knowledge of the staff was absolute. Paul visualised them once again, sitting together, the thin, elderly man in his shabby raincoat, and the exuberant, glowing girl. As if it were a film, he saw what he had scarcely registered at the time : Mr. Thomas's withdrawal from the touch of Hermione's body.

How terrible to be like that ! In a moment of perception, Paul knew that fear was the cause. It was a warning. Sally must be erased from his affections. Hermione was pretty and appealing, warm, and eager to please. He did not know her tastes, but he would soon find out what they were, and, if he did not share them, there were other girls, hundreds of them, all around, in mini-skirts and boots, in slacks and tailored jackets, all young, some alluring, and quite a lot of them available. Somewhere there must be one for him. He walked along The Grove, whistling.

Halfway down the road was Number 65, and as he drew level with it, the front door opened.

'Shut your trap, you bloody cow,' he heard. Then the door banged, footsteps sounded on the paved pathway, the rickety gate burst open, and the burly figure of Peter Betts blundered out into the roadway, muttering.

Paul paused. It would be awkward if they met head on. While he watched, Peter Betts fell, rather than got, into a shabby Vauxhall Viva that was parked outside his gate; he started the engine, slammed it into gear, and drove off at full tilt.

Bloody fool, thought Paul. He stood for a moment, irresolute, on the pavement, remembering what he had heard. Doubtfully, he glanced at the house. A light showed in a downstairs window, and all was quiet. He put his hand on the gate, debating whether to call; then he withdrew. It was not his business. Peter was tight, of course, but Marjorie must be used to that; it was probably just a squabble, and she would be embarrassed if she knew that he had witnessed the unpleasant incident.

He walked on up the road.

In the kitchen of Number 65, Marjorie stood by the stove, clasping her hand and moaning. Peter, before he left, had snatched the pan of boiling milk which she had put on for the children's cocoa and, deliberately, if with wobbling aim, poured it over her.

9

Sunday, for Joan Seabright, meant the luxury of a late start to the day. She sometimes slept till ten o'clock; though when one or both of her sons were at home the weekends were busy, with the flat full of young people wanting food, or simply a listener to their outpouring of talk. In term-time there was blessed peace and she revelled in it; it never lasted long enough to become boring. Her life ran predictably enough now; she enjoyed her job and had developed a satisfactory routine for coping with it and the demands of her sons. The early years, when the boys were small, had been tough; she looked back sometimes and marvelled at how she had weathered the storms. She was over the hump now; her elder son was reading physics; the younger, mathematics; if she opened any of their textbooks she could not understand a word of either, but she knew that in the technological world of tomorrow their futures would be safe. Roger had already announced his intention of letting his brain be lured across the Atlantic; he declared that she must follow and bask in the jet-age efficiency of a modern American home, or, better, trap an oil-man for herself.

'You're not bad-looking, Mum,' he conceded kindly, discussing the advantages of this idea.

Tom's aims were still vague. He might teach, or he might do research. They had grown into a pair of amiable youths, somewhat untidy, thoroughly absorbed in their own affairs, yet sparing time and some affection for their mother.

Joan had come a long way in a decade; no moper she, she had built for herself a new life after the wreck of her marriage; she had established her children on the threshold of good careers and made a place of some consequence for herself. Her job at Bliss's suited her well; she was efficient, and knew it. Bertram never asked the impossible, and he met her more than halfway over any problems; in the past there had been bouts of measles, the odd attack of flu, and various other domestic crises which kept her from her work, but those were over now and he reaped the benefit of past tolerance in her loyalty and sustained effort. To Bertram, she was worth every penny of her considerable salary; she undertook more and more responsibility, and it was only the knowledge that she would have to be replaced if he put her on the board, for she could no longer then be called his private secretary, that made him delay her promotion. It would come, and Joan knew it; she was content to wait.

She was drinking her second cup of coffee, still in her dressing-gown, when the telephone rang. It would probably be Geoffrey. He usually rang on Sunday morning if they had made no plans to meet. Geoffrey Hudson was a middle-aged bachelor, a quantity surveyor, with whom she maintained a friendship of a satisfying and undemanding nature which threatened the independence of neither.

But it was a female voice on the line; one she did not recognise. She was astonished when the caller identified herself as Marjorie Betts from Bliss's lighting department.

Joan made a swift mental adjustment. She knew Marjorie slightly; once or twice they had shared a table in the cafeteria, but she did not invite intimacy from any of the staff, for she considered herself to be on another and loftier plane than the saleswomen. Marjorie had always seemed appropriately humble; why was she suddenly so forward?

She was soon told.

'Please forgive me for disturbing you, and on a Sunday too,' Marjorie was apologising. 'I wondered if I could possibly come and see you for five minutes? It's very urgent.'

73

Joan frowned. Bliss's affairs were never allowed to intrude upon her weekends.

'It's not about the store. It's a personal matter,' Marjorie went on. 'I don't know anyone else who could help.'

Within Joan dread that she was to be asked to put herself out for another warred with gratification at being considered an oracle. After a short struggle common humanity won, for Mrs. Betts certainly sounded agitated.

'Of course. Come on over,' said Joan.

'Oh, thank you. I'll be half an hour or more,' Marjorie said. 'The buses don't start until midday. I'll have to walk.'

'Nor they do. Well, I'll be here all morning,' Joan said, putting warmth into her voice.

'Thank you very much, Mrs. Seabright. I'm so grateful.' Marjorie's voice quavered as she said this, and rang off. Joan was left irritably speculating about her problem. She quickly put on a pair of dark red slacks and a thick sweater and had just finished doing her face when the doorbell rang twenty minutes after Marjorie had telephoned.

'I'm earlier than I said. I met Mr. Jessamy and he gave me a lift,' Marjorie explained, standing in the doorway dressed in a shabby raincoat, with a pale blue scarf tied over her head.

'How lucky. Well, come along in and let me take your things,' Joan urged. She could see that Marjorie was somewhat distraught, and as she helped her off with her coat she noticed that her right hand was clumsily bandaged.

'What have you done to yourself?' asked Joan.

'It's a scald. It's partly why I've come,' Marjorie said. 'One of the reasons, at least.'

'Well, come in,' Joan said. She hung Marjorie's coat on a peg in the tiny hall and spread her scarf, which was very damp, over the back of a chair. 'Tell me what the trouble is.'

74

She led Marjorie into the living-room, which was warm and very tidy. No casually laid-down books, no knitting or mending, were visible, and the Sunday paper was neatly folded on the table. A large window looked out across the town, to the river, but the view was grey and rain-soaked this morning.

'Mr. Jessamy had Hermione Tipps with him,' said Marjorie conversationally. 'They've gone to Birdsea for the day. He's got a little boat there, it seems, and he's going to paint it. They took Michael and Amanda with them, just like that on the spur of the moment. Wasn't it kind?'

It was kind indeed. Several thoughts rushed into Joan's mind, and the first was amazement at Paul Jessamy's choice of Hermione Tipps as his companion.

'His parents have a hotel at Birdsea,' she said. 'I expect he goes over most weekends.'

Needless to say, Michael and Amanda had been thrilled at the prospect of the outing, and by the car ride, crammed into the tiny back space of Paul's ancient sports car. He had overtaken the trio as they trudged along in the rain, the children lagging behind their mother, dressed in raincoats and rubber boots and with Michael complaining because his toes were cramped. Marjorie had planned to leave them in the park, wet as it was, while she was with Joan. She would not leave them alone at home in case Peter came back in the same mood as when he had left the night before.

'Now, sit down, Mrs. Betts, and tell me how you hurt your hand,' prompted Joan, shepherding her guest towards the sofa.

It was an effort for Marjorie to begin her tale, but when at last she started to explain it was as though a dam had burst. Words poured from her in a torrent, some incoherent, but in the main her story hung together, all too possible, patently true. Joan said very little, merely

75

putting in an occasional query when Marjorie lost the thread of her narrative.

'I knew you were divorced, and you've got children,' Marjorie said at the end. 'I don't know anyone else who is. I thought you might be able to tell me what to do.'

She sat back, drained.

Joan got up.

'I think we could both use a drink,' she said, and went to a bow-fronted corner cupboard from which she took bottles and glasses. Without consulting Marjorie, she poured each of them a brandy and ginger ale.

Marjorie took her glass without protest. It was as if, with her confidences, she had totally surrendered herself to the other woman's initiative.

'I'm glad you did come, but I can't advise you,' Joan said. 'You must make up your own mind what to do.'

'Well, you see, if I leave him, where can we go? What can we do? How shall we manage? Amanda's at the High School, and I hope Michael's going to get into the Grammar School. My parents are dead, so we can't go to them.' And they would be aghast, too, if alive, to think their daughter could contemplate the dissolution of her marriage.

'But you want to leave? You're sure of that?'

'How can I go on?' Marjorie asked.

She had chosen, in fact. By seeking this interview she had proved that, Joan realised, and became more definite.

'You need legal advice, and somewhere else to live,' she said. 'Somewhere in this area, I suggest, so that the children can stay at their schools and keep their friends, and where you've got your job already.' She thought for a minute. 'What about that hand of yours, has a doctor seen it?'

'No. I bathed it with bicarbonate and Amanda bandaged it. I told her I'd done it myself, accidentally, of course.'

Joan said: 'If you're to bring a divorce case for cruelty, or constructive desertion, you'll need evidence. This hand is evidence. You can't lock him out of the house, I suppose, so if you leave it's constructive desertion because his treatment has forced you to go.'

Marjorie looked bewildered.

'I didn't know there was such a thing,' she said.

'There is, but it's better if you can sue for cruelty. It's quicker,' said Joan bluntly. 'The other takes three years, but you'd have to do it if there isn't enough evidence for cruelty. However, you've got plenty, I'd say.'

'He'd say he hadn't meant to do it. He'd deny it,' said Marjorie.

'And everything else? All that you've just told me?' demanded Joan. 'Who will the court believe, you or him? I know who I would.' She remembered back, ten years before. Things then had been, for her, so little different from Marjorie's present plight, but during that time the climate of opinion had changed; divorce was no longer such a rare and humiliating event.

She said: 'No one should have to tolerate such degradation. You haven't had a marriage, you've been in serfdom to a bully. Come out into the twentieth century. It's far better to live alone than in such misery, however difficult. Your kids will think so too, one day. They can't be blind. They must have an idea of how things are.'

'They don't see Peter much. They're usually in bed when he gets back,' Marjorie offered.

'I thought my two didn't notice anything, because we didn't fight in front of them,' Joan said. 'A few years ago they told me they used to lie in bed and hear us, when we thought they were asleep. Atmosphere tells on kids. They feel the tension.' She brooded. 'I'm older than you. There are times when one just has to put up with things and hang on, like in the war, or with illness; you haven't the

77

power to improve them. But this is different; something can be done to make it better all round.'

Marjorie knew that it would be impossible to remain in the house and lock Peter out. Last night, after the children had gone to bed, she had thought about this, but fear of the noise he would make and the resulting scene and disturbance had prevented her from doing what every instinct prompted. For the same reason, when at length he had blundered into their room and flung himself into the bed where she lay, rigid, at the furthermost edge, she had muffled the cry of protest that rose to her throat now whenever the monstrous invasion threatened. She was filled with loathing and disgust; but more than this, she feared him. When sober, he could turn on charm like a tap; this he did for Amanda and Michael, rarely now, but sometimes; perhaps the ability was waning. It was what had deceived her in the beginning; it was never assumed for her now. Last night, after the first unbearable minutes while he mauled at her with grasping hands and seeking body, rescue came. Cursing, blaming her lack of response for his own inadequacy, he flung her from him, crawled off the bed and stumbled out of the room. She had heard the car start up a short time later. He had not come back. She knew that she could not bear to have his touch upon her ever again.

Joan was talking.

'He may have someone else tucked away. That would make it a lot easier,' she said. 'Has he, do you think?'

'I've no idea. It's possible, I suppose. He's away a lot.'

'Let's hope he has. Well, the first thing to do is to get your hand seen to and properly witnessed. You must tell the doctor just what happened,' Joan said. 'It will be a damned good thing when they change the law to grant divorce when a marriage has irretrievably broken down, without appointing the blame.'

'I suppose they mustn't make it too easy,' Marjorie said.

78

'No one gets divorced in a fit of pique, not this side of the Atlantic, anyway,' said Joan. 'It's a hell of a business, whatever you do.' And you just wait, she thought : wait till you've dredged through the mire with your lawyers, digging up half-forgotten episodes and insults, resurrecting bitterness and making sure of more; better by far a quiet interment, with restricted acrimony.

She got up and went to the telephone. Her doctor had a daughter Tom's age, and the families had become friends; he agreed to see Marjorie at once, and accordingly they set off in Joan's small yellow Fiat.

The doctor was kind and attentive; he dressed the hand and asked Marjorie if she thought her husband had deliberately intended to hurt her; when she said yes, he remarked, 'Hmph, not nice. Not nice at all.'

Afterwards, driving back, Joan said : 'Doctors hate giving evidence in cases like this, but he'll do it. That's why I took you to him. Don't worry.'

By this time Marjorie felt as if she were in a dream. None of this could really be happening to her, Marjorie Betts; it was totally unreal. Apart from emotional shock, she was suffering from the effects of a strong brandy on virtually an empty stomach, for before reaching Joan's she had had only a cup of tea since lunch on the previous day. Lunch, after Mr. Bliss had brought her home : it was only twenty-four hours ago, yet it seemed like a week. She sat in Joan's car in a trance, but when they reached the block of flats she made an effort.

'I must go now. You've been wonderfully kind, Mrs. Seabright.'

'Nonsense. You're coming in to have something to eat, and then we'll hatch a plan,' said Joan briskly. All thought of remaining uninvolved had fled; she was in this now, up to her neck, and must see it through.

She had two small chops in the refrigerator. Eked out with vegetables from tins they made a meal for two.

Marjorie, astonishingly, found that she was ravenous; she meekly ate what was put before her, and followed up the meat with a banana and some bread and cheese, then a cup of strong coffee.

While they drank their coffee, Joan read aloud to Marjorie selections from the 'To Let' column of the local paper.

'But I'll never manage!' Marjorie exclaimed. 'I earn nine pounds a week. It'll never stretch.'

Peter had not given her much, but he had paid the mortgage, the rates and the fuel at least, and occasionally flung her some money at the start of the month.

'You will. You'll know where you are, and that's a beginning,' said Joan firmly. 'Your husband will have to give you something, maintenance for the children at least, though he'll probably wangle out of paying much for you. He'll plead poverty and say you're earning. But he can't escape total responsibility for his kids, no matter what. You might be able to pull in some more, if you could put in longer hours; you might move up a bit, in time. What did you do before you were married?'

'I was a secretary.' Far-off years: Marjorie could hardly recall what it had been like in those distant days in the calm council offices of her home town where she had worked before Peter appeared in her life. 'But I couldn't do that now. I've forgotten it all. And I couldn't do a longer day. As it is, I arrive late and leave early from the store, because of the children.'

'They're getting older. You'll manage more soon,' said Joan. A plan, long-term but excellent, had come to her. 'I think you must tell Mr. Bliss what's happened. He'll help.'

'Oh dear!' Marjorie was dismayed by this advice.

'It's the best thing to do. He's marvellous about this sort of thing,' said Joan, who dealt constantly with problems arising among the personnel at the store and knew how practical Bertram's aid could be. 'There's a fund that you could borrow from, if necessary. Lots of people have problems; you aren't the only one.'

'Oh, I know!' Marjorie hastily disclaimed the uniqueness of her position.

'Why don't you let me tell him the bare bones tomorrow?' Joan suggested. 'He knows everyone in Sedgemouth, he'll know which solicitor you should go to. Don't forget,' and she quoted, ' "We're one big family at Bliss's." Take advantage of having the store behind you. It'll make your husband think twice, too, if he knows Mr. Bliss is on your side.'

'Well, if you think it's the best thing . . .' Marjorie had very little will of her own left now.

'Good. That's settled, then,' said Joan. She frowned over the newspaper which she still held in her hand. 'I don't like the idea of your going back, though, to face another round in the battle, even if it does give you more fuel for evidence. You can't do it.'

Marjorie agreed, but saw no alternative. She had thirty pounds saved in the Post Office; that was all. Yet how could she find the strength to face Peter again?

'You must all come here for the time being,' Joan decided. 'Till we can find you a place.' Valiantly she laid aside her cherished solitude. 'You and Amanda can have the boys' room, and Michael can sleep in here. It'll only be for a few days, to give us time to look about.' She thought that if Marjorie went back to her daily routine she would either be murdered at her post or would sink into spiritless passivity and never break out again. 'We'll get Paul on the telephone and tell him to bring the children here.'

'They're going to be badly hurt by this,' Marjorie said. 'It's always the children who suffer.'

'That's a cliché. What about the poor parents, in thrall to them?' Joan demanded. 'Yes, they'll suffer from having separated parents, but they're suffering now from having a nervous wreck of a mother and a tyrannical father. Which do you choose?'

'I'm not like you. You're tough,' Marjorie said. 'I'm a coward!'

'I wasn't always like this,' said Joan. 'Once I cringed too. You'll be surprised how soon you mend. You'll discover yourself as an individual, and that's worth doing. I expect you married too young to have achieved your real identity. You wait, you'll be a much better person for your kids, after a bit. You'll see.'

'Peter might take them away. The children, I mean.'

'I doubt it. He wouldn't want the bother of them. Oh, he'll insist on his rights, he'll take them out and spoil them, just to spite you. But he'll give up the moment they become a nuisance. They'll play you off against each other, I expect; bound to. But they'll get used to it and so will you. And you'll be fit only for a bin if you go on like this much longer.'

'I know.' Marjorie's little flame of doubt flickered out. She sat twisting her hands together, playing with her wedding-ring as if it irritated her finger.

'The children will sort it out as they get older,' Joan said, more gently. 'Mine have. We had our ups and downs, but they always knew they could depend on me. Their father promised them this and that, and then let them down. Now they just go and see him when they want to touch him for a quid or two. He's done well for himself. It used to shock me, such mercenary conduct, but I accept it now. It's a lot healthier than morbid brooding, and if they can squeeze a few pounds out of him, good luck to them. Why should I worry? Come on, we'll go over and collect your toothbrushes and things.'

She's hard, Marjorie thought. Goodness, she's hard. But it was toughen or sink, she realised. She took a breath. She had better start right away.

'What if Peter's come back?'

What indeed? Joan thought.

Aloud, she said: 'We'll face that if it happens. I'll be there. I doubt if he'll do much if you're not alone.'

It was true. In front of other people he was often sweetness and light personified.

But Peter was not at the house. Quickly, the two women packed the children's clothes, emptying the drawers straight into cases. They piled loose objects into corners of the car: a football and a hockey stick; satchels; a cricket bat. Marjorie snatched up as many of her own possessions as they could cram in on top.

'Should I leave him a note?' she asked, pausing in the hall before they left.

'Why? It's obvious you've gone,' Joan said. 'Come on. We must hurry.'

She feared they would still be there when Peter returned; their luck might not last. She was afraid, too, that Marjorie might weaken and fall prey to sentimentality.

But she did not. She caught up Amanda's teddy bear, worn shabby by much cherishing, banged the door shut, and followed Joan to the car without a backward glance.

10

The Sunday trains from Paddington to Sedgemouth were few, and slow. However, there was a restaurant car, where lunch whiled away some of the time. Bertram read steadily through *The Observer* and *The Sunday Times,* supplements too; Shirley glanced at the gossip and the women's pages in *The Sunday Express,* and wished she had brought her library book, a gothic romance by a favourite author. After lunch she slept for half an hour, her mouth a little open and her face flushed. Bertram frowned irritably as a tiny snore escaped her; fortunately they were alone in the compartment.

Last night's theatre had been pleasant entertainment. They had seen a musical play that had been running for some months; the tunes were gay and the pace brisk; no great effort was required in order to enjoy it. Nicely stimulated, they had eaten a good dinner afterwards, which had cost much more than Bertram thought it was worth. When they were back at their hotel, undressing together in the intimacy of their room, Shirley was impelled to tell Bertram that she had seen Sally early in the evening.

'She was with a man, arm-in-arm,' Shirley said. 'He looked rather distinguished. Perhaps she's going to get married.' Most of the time, Shirley considered this to be women's prime function and best aim; only occasionally did she wonder what it was like to be free, and run your own life according to your talents.

'I hope not.' Bertram answered instantly, without thought.

'Why not? I suppose you don't want her to leave?'

'That's right.' He snatched at this reason. He put on his pyjamas at maximum speed and climbed into his own allotted bed, where he immediately closed his eyes. Across his lids there at once arose a misty image of Sally, clasped in the arms of a man of indeterminate but distinguished aspect. Bertram rubbed his hand across his eyes to blot it out, but it would not be erased. He tried to think about the play they had just seen, even mentally to hum a tune from it, but these tricks did no good. It was Sally that he saw in his mind's eye, elusive, enchanting, and now, it seemed, perhaps already lost.

Shirley creamed her face, wiped it with a tissue, brushed

out her long hair now released from its knot and quickly twisted it into its nightly plait. She hurried these ritual tasks, but not too obviously. At last she was ready. With an unromantic creak of springs she got into bed.

'Thank you for a lovely evening, darling,' she tried, and stretched out an arm across the dividing gangway between them.

There was no response.

Now, half-dozing in the train, she remembered this. Of course, Bertie was tired, and not so young any more. She could not find it in her heart to chide him, even silently; still, it was a pity. Well, tomorrow at least held something she could look forward to; Bliss's fashions were in her charge.

It was Bertram who saw Sally at Sedgemouth station. She was walking along the platform from the rear end of the train; she must have travelled in the last coach. After Shirley's disclosure of the night before he had hoped she might be on this train, and had unobtrusively looked for her at Paddington, but in vain. Since it was Sunday, there were no porters, and he was perforce burdened with his own and Shirley's cases; nevertheless, when Sally came through the barrier, he was waiting, hat off exposing his thin, sandy hair, with a hand to spare for her small bag.

'My dear Sally, what a happy meeting!' he cried. 'You must let me drive you home.'

Sally had planned to get a taxi, and blow the cost. She was surprised to see Mr. Bliss; when he spoke to her her mind was far away with Derek in Wimbledon, where by now he would be in the midst of a family Sunday with his wife and two small sons. It took her a minute to adjust to the physical manifestation here of her employer. Then she saw Shirley, beaming genially in the background.

It would be ungracious to refuse the offer of a lift, and Shirley's presence made a difference. She got into the back of the Rover and made only token protest at the inconvenience to Bertram of driving out to Warren End, in completely the opposite direction to Castle Hill. But when the car glided slowly to a halt at her gate, of course she was obliged to ask Mr. and Mrs. Bliss to come inside.

Shirley demurred, but Bertram sprang from the car, all eager acceptance.

Sally opened the heavy oak door and led them into a square-flagged hall where an oak dower chest stood, with a bowl of hyacinths in bud upon it. Two pleasant water-colours of pastoral scenes hung on the white walls. As they followed Sally, a door opened at the end of the hall and her father came out of his study, his spectacles on and the paper in his hand.

Shirley had not met Sally's father before. He was a sturdily built man, with thick grey hair now rather untidy, and he wore an old, lovat-coloured cardigan and shabby grey flannels. Sally introduced them, and Shirley mur-mured some apology about disturbing Mr. Manners' Sunday afternoon.

'Come into the sitting-room,' said Sally, leading the way into another room that led off the hall. 'Oh, Daddy, you are naughty, you haven't lit the fire,' she scolded.

The room was, indeed, chilly, in spite of a radiator along one wall. Shirley suppressed the slight shiver she felt, despite her mink, as she entered. The fire was laid in the grate, and Sally crouched before it and applied a match. Paper and sticks soon crackled cheerfully.

'There, that's better,' said Sally. 'Now, watch it, Daddy, while I put the kettle on,' she instructed, and left the room.

Bertram at once began to praise Sally to her father in fulsome terms, while Shirley sat quietly, looking about her. There were some good pieces of furniture in the room, a walnut tallboy and a round, rosewood table now piled with books. The carpet was worn in places, and the blue brocade curtains were bleached at their edges from the sunlight. The atmosphere was tranquil; these things had

86

grown together with the years, haphazardly assembled as occasion offered, yet blending now. Shirley wondered why she had shivered when she first came in, and thought fancifully that she must have felt the gentle ghost of Mrs. Manners haunting the home she had made. She looked at Sally's father, who was listening to Bertram's explanation of how they had met at the station.

'Sally often goes up to stay with a school friend who's got her hands full with three small children,' said Mr. Manners. 'It's nice for them to keep in touch, and does Sally good to get away. She spends too much time with me, bless her.'

A glance passed between Bertram and Shirley : surprise, doubt, complicity. Both realised there was something to conceal and for different reasons resolved to aid the deception. Mr. Manners went on talking. He spoke sympathetically about the troubles of Miss Westcott, whom he had met once or twice when seeking out Sally in the store.

'Though I don't usually venture further than the men's department, Mr. Bliss,' he added with a smile. 'I buy all my shirts from your excellent Mr. Thomas.'

'I hope you get Sally to pay for them, and use her discount,' said Bertram at once.

'Why, no. I couldn't do that,' said Mr. Manners.

'Why not? I assure you, you should,' Bertram said, and when Sally returned, wheeling the tea-trolley, he challenged her.

'I know, Mr. Bliss. I've told him often enough,' she declared, with a wry glance at her parent who now looked sheepish, caught in the full blaze of his exposed integrity.

'I think you're amazing, Mr. Manners, in these days of grasp and get,' Shirley said. 'It does me good to hear you. All the same, please stop buying at full rates. We can stand it.'

At this, Mr. Manners laughed, and his lined face

looked suddenly younger. Of course, he was much the same age as Bertram.

'If you say so, Mrs. Bliss, I yield,' he said. 'Let's change the subject. How was Phoebe, Sally?'

'What? Oh, fine.' Sally for an instant looked cornered; then she recovered and began an involved explanation about her friend and her friend's three children, and her husband in advertising.

'And I suppose they live in a flat in Kensington?' Bertram slyly asked.

'No. They've a tiny house in Putney, near the Common,' Sally said. 'It's nice for the boys to be able to rampage about there, and the dog. Ideal, really.'

'Yes, it must be,' Shirley said. She looked at Sally with new understanding, and saw the shadows under her eyes, her too-thin wrists, her taut manner. There was trouble here.

As they left, Bertram repeated the dinner invitation for the night of the store's Christmas dance, which Sally had earlier received. Mr. Manners, when first told of it, had hedged. He did not want to bother with the social life of Bliss's, and thought Sally would have more fun if he was absent; but now he changed his mind, and accepted. Mr. and Mrs. Bliss were his contemporaries; they thought well of his Sally, and he had enjoyed their brief visit; he should make more effort to get out and about. He might even take up golf again, long abandoned in the years of Mary's illness. When the Blisses had gone he stood in the hall and swung an imaginary club. Then he wandered away, back to his study, where a slow combustion stove burned night and day, and a black cat slept on the hearth.

Sally propelled the trolley out to the kitchen and piled the china with a clatter in the sink.

Where do we go from here? she thought, as she always did now after being with Derek. Gone was the first ecstatic joy; she was deeply tangled, bound with webs of

88

lies and subterfuge, one of the multitude who must make do with crumbs for comfort. Her eyes burned with unshed tears as fiercely she washed the cups and saucers, scraping away at Shirley's crimson lipstick print. On Sundays after tea Derek read to his children or played halma with them. They went to bed at seven, and then the evening stretched ahead, alone with Angela. The evening, and the night.

She could not bear to think of it, and closed her mind. As she savagely dried the dishes, one of the saucers fell from her hand and broke in three pieces on the floor. She picked up the biggest bit and flung it down again, hard, on the red tiles. It shattered into fragments which flew all around the room.

It took her several minutes to make sure she had swept up every splinter.

II

Behind a door labelled *Women* on the top floor of Bliss's store was the large cloakroom where most of the female staff hung their coats, kept spare shoes and shopping bags in lockers, powdered their faces, swallowed aspirins and exchanged gossip and confidences. At the peak hours of nine in the morning and five-thirty in the afternoon it was a seething mass of girls and women.

Hermione Tipps arrived early on the Monday morning after her day with Paul at Birdsea. She had caught the bus before her usual one, having discovered over the weekend that Paul always reached the store at eight-forty-five. When he boarded the bus, there she was, already seated, beaming at him. They walked together down the street to the staff entrance, ignoring Mr. Thomas who followed ten paces behind. Inside the door they parted, for the apartment assigned to *Men* was in the basement. Hermione, singing gaily, went along to the lift, rose aloft, and bounced jauntily down the corridor in her tall brown boots. She dawdled about, adding extra blue to her eyelids and admiring her curves in the mirror that stretched down one wall of the cloakroom. Today she wore a brief green skirt and darker green tights; her mane of blonde hair was held back in a black velvet bow.

She was happy. Paul had been amused, not cross, when her small deception about where she lived was discovered. At any rate, he had kissed her lightly on the mouth and invited her to spend the day with him on Sunday. She had been somewhat put about when he stopped for Mrs. Betts and the children; she was still more disconcerted when he suggested the youngsters should go with them to Birdsea, and sulked for several miles. But Mrs. Betts did look bad, white-faced and as if she'd been crying, and she'd hurt her hand. So Paul was right, really; it showed all the more what a beautiful nature he had. When they reached Birdsea she soon cheered up, for though the weather was damp and dull the sea air was invigorating. They scraped the hull of Paul's boat industriously in what was left of the morning. Michael got down to the job with a will, though Amanda soon grew bored. She and Hermione went off for a walk by the water's edge, leaving the men to their labours. They strolled along, watching the gulls swoop and hearing their calls. The sea was grey and still; the houses were quiet, windows tight shut, paintwork dulled by spray. In summer this would be a gay scene, with dozens of boats in the water, beach huts in use, the houses and hotels refurbished and bustling.

Paul's parents produced a fabulous lunch in their hotel. Hermione felt timid about meeting them, but they were too busy to be critical of her. In winter local people who kept away in the season filled the hotel for meals. Hermione ate with healthy appetite, and so did the children. Afterwards Paul took them round the harbour in an outboard dinghy. The sun appeared feebly during this trip; the little boat puttered along and a proud Michael was allowed to take the helm. Then the clouds closed down again and, as they came back to the hotel, rain began to fall. Paul's mother greeted them with a message that the Betts children were to be dropped at Mrs. Seabright's flat.

It was rather mysterious. Michael and Amanda did not seem puzzled that their mother had clearly spent the day in the tall new block of flats near the bridge. But Hermione found it strange; she heard most of the gossip in the store and did not know that the toffee-nosed Mrs. Seabright and meek Mrs. Betts were friends.

Paul had taken Hermione home and stayed for cold ham and pickles with her parents. After he left they commented upon him in favourable terms and Hermione was filled with young, resurgent hope.

She added a layer of pale lipstick to her small, full mouth; then, as the cloakroom began to fill with the press of everyone else arriving, she cut her way through the incoming tide of female bodies with their odour of cosmetics, damp raincoats and sheer femininity, and sauntered down the passage to the office. As she passed the lift, Mrs. Seabright emerged; she smiled at Hermione and said 'Good morning', in what the girl thought of as her proud way, then walked briskly down the corridor in her black patents, crossed from the lino zone on to the pale carpeting, and vanished from sight.

Joan did not feel her normal poised self today; it had been a great scramble in the flat this morning. She had found Michael shining his shoes on the top of her sofatable. Then Amanda had knocked over her cocoa at

91

breakfast; she liked neither coffee nor tea, and Joan's milk supply was inadequate for such extra demands, so that Michael had been sent down the road to a milk-vending machine which was luckily near. The children were obedient, but their docile acceptance of the night before had turned to bewilderment this morning. They would not be fobbed off for long with the tale that they were staying while Marjorie's hand healed; if she could do a day's work in the store they would reason that she could manage at home. Michael had picked up his cricket bat and looked at it curiously, then out of the window at the dark, November day.

Well, first things first : the mail must be dealt with and urgent matters got out of the way before Mr. Bliss could be involved in Marjorie's troubles and applied to for aid. After a night's sleep Joan's crusading zeal had waned; she was anxious to enlist reinforcements.

In the cloakroom, Marjorie fought through the throng scarcely aware of the tumult; she was still dazed, carrying her isolation like a shell wrapped round her. Shielding her bandaged hand against her body, she was carried with the flow of emerging women out into the passage as they went to their various departments. The lift was soon full. Most of the assistants moved off down the stairs, clattering on the linoleum with their variegated shoes, some in high spike heels, some with stubby ones, some with soft old pumps on flat, spread feet. Marjorie, winding her way down, tread by tread, was surrounded by a babble of high, shrill voices. A few older women with whom she was friendly spoke to her and showed concern about her hand; it throbbed this morning. It should really be raised in a sling; she would try to rest it today. Joan had suggested she take a day or two off, till it felt better, but Marjorie wanted the security of Bliss's around her. Left alone, she would panic.

She felt calmer when she saw Paul Jessamy, already in

his little office. They exchanged their customary morning greeting and he asked about her injury.

'Let me know if you want any help. Don't go carrying things round,' he urged. Goodness, she looked awful; she couldn't be forty yet, but she looked like a woman of fifty today. 'Are you sure you're all right?' he asked. In spite, or perhaps because, of Hermione's curiosity, he had given vague replies to her guesses about the Betts family, uttered when the children had been dropped the night before; he was convinced he knew what had happened.

'Oh, I'm quite all right, thank you. Just a bit tired,' Marjorie said. 'Mr. Jessamy . . .' she began, and then paused.

'Yes, Mrs. Betts?'

'No, it's nothing.' The urge to confide was suppressed; self-revelation was mere self-indulgence. Everyone had troubles and no one wanted to be bothered by those of others. She walked to her corner, opened a cupboard and began to arrange a display of lampshades on her counter top.

Shirley Bliss heard nothing of the Betts affray until after lunchtime. She took her hour late, waiting until Maud Wilson returned at half past one. She still felt rather shy in the cafeteria, and always peered anxiously round in search of a friendly face. Bertram, forced to accept the fact of her presence in the store until Eileen came back, urged her to have a tray sent to his office, as he did, but she would not agree, for she said that the girls sometimes wanted to change their times around and she liked to be flexible. In fact, she never felt comfortable in Bertram's office. It was so bare and formal, so stark and austere. She had much preferred the cosy clutter of the little room from which Hawkins' Hardware had for so long been administered.

Today Joan Seabright was sitting in a corner of the cafeteria when Shirley arrived, smoking a cigarette over a cup of coffee. Marjorie Betts was beside her. While Shirley collected cottage pie and carrots, and steamed syrup pudding, Marjorie left, so that Joan was alone when Shirley approached the part of the room where by common consent most of the older and more senior staff sat.

'Do join me, Mrs. Bliss, won't you?' Joan invited, and Shirley set down her tray on the pale green formica. She made a resolution that during her spell in the store she would fight to overcome her awe of Joan. Now Joan's dark hair was neat, not a strand straying; her complexion was matt; her eyes, which were brown, were lightly shadowed with turquoise; her nails were varnished. Shirley knew that her own face shone; her knot of hair had loosened to let a few wisps straggle on her neck; her hands showed her age.

While she ate her cottage pie, Shirley replied to civil questions from Joan about the weekend just spent by Mr. and Mrs. Bliss in London. They discussed the theatre, then the films they had recently seen. It transpired that both were keen cinema-goers. When Joan confessed to a nostalgia for Ray Milland, now only to be seen in ancient movies on television, Shirley spoke of Herbert Lom. She began to relax; Mrs. Seabright was human, after all.

'And there's always Sir Ralph,' sighed Joan. 'Somehow he's so reassuring. It must mean something.' She stubbed out her cigarette in an imperfect pottery ashtray. Then she said: 'Mrs. Bliss, I do think you're splendid, standing in for Miss Westcott. I hope you don't mind my mentioning it.'

'Oh, no. Thank you.' Shirley looked flustered. 'To be truthful, I don't think Bertie approves, but I just love coming into the store,' she said. 'I've a lot of time on my hands, you see, having no family. Your sons must be a comfort, Mrs. Seabright.'

'Well, yes, but a worry too,' Joan said. 'They've been around for so long, about half my life, that I can't imagine what it would be like without them, but I assure you there have been times when I'd cheerfully have wrung both their necks.'

'I know you're joking,' Shirley said.

'Well, I suppose so.' Joan thought that Shirley Bliss was a nice woman. Few in her position would remain so unassuming. Surely some permanent niche could be found for her, high in the store status stakes, if she wanted it? But Joan understood her employer: he would think it unfitting and indicative of failure.

She said: 'Children leave home in the end. And one can't live their lives for them. An interest outside the family is good for everyone, even if it isn't needed financially. You could start a business of your own, a boutique of some sort. They're all the vogue now.'

'Oh, Mrs. Seabright, whatever would Bertie say?' Shirley asked. 'I'd take trade from Bliss's.'

'You could keep it very expensive and special, carrying lines outside our scope,' Joan suggested, interested to see how Shirley's face had softened into amusement at her idea. She must have been quite attractive as a girl, before she started to put on weight.

'Clothes, you mean?'

'Yes, or *objets d'art*—prints and so on. There's a big demand for such things and we haven't the space for an art department.'

Shirley said: 'What a lovely dream.'

'Someone will do it one day,' Joan pointed out. 'Sedgemouth is expanding all the while. There's plenty of room for competition.'

After she left, Shirley tackled her syrup pudding in solitude. What fun it would be to have her own little shop, just something small, but exclusive as Mrs. Seabright had said. And she knew that customers would flock to her; that very morning she had sold a tweed suit to the president of her own Floral Art Society. Instead of being shocked, as Bertie had foretold, at being served by the chairman's wife, Lady Murcott had spied Shirley and hailed her with cries of delight, eager to be dealt with by someone she knew and registering the very opposite of dismay.

She finished her meal and went along to the cloakroom set aside for the women heads of department. It was separated from the main cloakroom by a partition that ended short of the ceiling, and a babble of sound now flowed over this division. As Shirley set about doing her face, she could hear one particular conversation that carried louder than the rest.

'. . . hit her on the head and laid her out,' said a voice.

'I don't believe it !' said another.

'It's true. She's black and blue all over. So she's left him, and taken the kids.'

'Well, good for her. No one should put up with that. I'd hit him back.'

'Me too.'

Plugs pulled and water flushed. Shirley concluded her own operations; adding powder seemed only to create a translucent veil through which she still gleamed as before. The voices went on in the background, discussing some marital collapse, but Shirley was not really listening.

When she got back to the department Maud Wilson and another of the girls were huddled together talking earnestly. They broke apart as Shirley approached, and she heard Maud say, 'Poor Mrs. Betts,' but before she could ask what was wrong a customer came in, and everything else left her mind.

At four o'clock Sally appeared. She wanted a red coat and suit for the window. Maud was busy, so Shirley went with her to the rack and watched her make a choice.

'I love that colour,' she said, as Sally took out a mohair coat, simply cut, in a deep, rich crimson.

'It would suit you, Mrs. Bliss,' said Sally.

'Oh, no. I'd look like a beetroot, red all over with my red face,' said Shirley.

'It would set off your hair and your eyes,' Sally said. 'Why don't you treat yourself to a new red dress for the dance?' The words were lightly said, a throwaway remark that sprang from mere civility, but Shirley took it up.

'Shall I try one? I must get something new, of course. I was forgetting.' Traditionally she always wore a new dress for the dance; nothing, however becoming, that had been seen before must appear, by Bertie's decree.

'You do that, and see if I'm not right,' Sally encouraged. 'This is nice, don't you think?' She picked out another coat. 'What else shall I put in the window, Mrs. Bliss?'

They talked about it, and Sally tried one coat on. The other was in a larger size.

'You put it on, and show me how it looks,' Sally said, and so Shirley did, parading in front of the mirror. She found that the girl was right; the colour made her look paler. Her fine, dark eyes shone. She did not see Bertie pass by in the distance while she was engaged in this little interlude. Sally at last decided what to put on the dummies, and they returned the other garments to the rail. Both were enjoying themselves.

'It was nice meeting your father, Sally,' Shirley said. 'Thank you for giving us tea.'

'It was nice for us,' said Sally. 'Father enjoyed it, it did him good. He doesn't see many people apart from those at work. He gave up so much when my mother was ill, and he's never picked up his old friends again. I'm glad he's coming to the dance.'

'Oh, so am I,' said Shirley. 'Poor man, it's so sad. And for you, too, Sally.'

'It's always the people who'll most be missed who seem to die early,' said Sally.

'My dear!' Shirley did not know how to answer.

'Well, now there's poor Mrs. Betts—have you heard?'
Sally was away, borne off on the torrent of one of her
enthusiasms. 'Her husband knocks her about. Well, he
went too far over the weekend, so she's left him. He won't
die, though. He'll haunt her for the rest of her life, even
if she divorces him and marries someone else. She'll never
be really rid of him.'

'Sally is this true? Are you sure?'

'Yes. She's taken the children away and they're staying
with Mrs. Seabright,' Sally said. 'Wendy heard about it
at lunchtime.'

'I had lunch with Mrs. Seabright and she never mentioned it,' said Shirley.

'She probably thought you already knew,' said Sally.
'The jungle drums don't waste much time spreading news
as a rule. Look, is it all right if I take this other coat too?
On second thoughts, I'll put an extra figure in the
window.'

'Yes, dear, of course. It's so pretty that someone will
probably buy it right away,' said Shirley.

'Good for business,' said Sally. She hung the thick,
expensive coats over her arm and hurried off. Shirley
stood still, stupefied, for several seconds, taking in what
she had heard.

12

The news had leaked quite simply. After Joan had told
Bertram the story of the weekend's events, he telephoned
Paul in the household department, asking for Mrs. Betts
to be sent up to the chairman's office.

'Bad business, Paul. Her husband's been knocking her

about, it seems.' His voice was stern, deeper than usual; tough, man to man, was his mood.

'Is that so?' Paul spoke guardedly, peering through his little window across the department. Masked by tall standerd lamps hung with fringed shades, Marjorie could be discerned, softly illumined among her wares.

'Mrs. Seabright has been putting me in the picture. We must come to the rescue,' said Bertram firmly. Gone was the merry grocer of his imagination; a bewhiskered ape-man with fleshy jowls replaced him as an incarnation of Mr. Betts.

'Of course. Can I help at all?'

'Very probably. Come up later and we'll have a chat,' said Bertram. 'Mrs. Seabright's been extremely good, taking them in, but this won't be the end of it, mark my words.'

'I'm sure you're right,' said Paul. He had been hourly expecting Mr. Betts to arrive in the department cracking a large whip and demanding the return of his wife. He must surely react in some violent fashion.

'She'll need legal assistance,' Bertram was saying.

'Yes. I'll send her up right away,' said Paul.

Ivy Smith at the switchboard, having few lines busy, was free to listen to this conversation. She was naturally agog at what she heard, and soon spread the tale upon its way. With each telling it grew more extravagant. The version Shirley heard was mild compared with some.

Bertram arrived home great with tidings to pass on to Shirley; he had rehearsed a history in which his own role as wise father confessor loomed large. It was deflating to find that she had already heard what had happened.

'Mr. Manners is a solicitor, isn't he?' Shirley said. 'Couldn't he help?'

'That's a good idea,' said Bertram. 'It would keep it all in the family, so to speak. Much better that way, poor woman.'

Shirley could not stop thinking about the Betts children. They must love both their parents and this was terrible.

'The man's a brute, of course,' Bertram said. 'I'll ask Manners round after dinner. Perhaps Sally will come too.'

'Isn't Sally better left out of it?' Shirley said. 'After all, it's Mrs. Betts's most intimate life that's involved. It's not really anything to do with Sally.'

There was logic here. Bertram would not argue; he slid sideways.

'Perhaps you're right,' he conceded. He picked up the telephone. Instead of asking Mr. Manners to call, he proposed going over himself to Warren End later that evening.

Shirley walked heavily upstairs. She must change from her working jersey dress into something more *chic,* even if Bertie would be at home only briefly. She was tired. She was no longer used to hard physical work, but she would not confess her fatigue, for Bertie would merely say he had told her she shouldn't do it. She put on a brown dress with a fur collar and old, stretched shoes, and then carefully made up her face before going downstairs to prepare the dinner.

When Bertram reached the house at Warren End, Sally was not to be seen. Mr. Manners appeared pleased, if surprised, at seeing Bertram again so soon. He led the way into his study, which was cosy and snug; there were deep leather chairs, and bookshelves lined the walls.

'Sally's gone to the cinema,' he said. He produced a bottle of brandy, and the two men sat holding their balloon glasses on opposite sides of the fire, with the sleek black cat stretched out between them on the hearthrug.

Bertram told his tale.

Mr. Manners listened in silence, and did not speak for a minute after Bertram had ceased. Then he said, 'Poor woman, it's not an unusual story, I'm afraid, but it's tricky. Of course I'll see her. I suppose she'll want a divorce. Cruelty cases are always difficult; give me a good clean adultery any day. With any luck this fellow has got someone else tucked away.'

'I really don't know.' Bertram was taken aback at this attitude.

'So much raking up of old grievances goes on in a cruelty case,' Mr. Manners explained. 'Every old slight and sore is remembered and resurrected. But still, physical violence can be proved in this case, which helps. It's harder when all the torture has been mental. What a good thing she consulted a doctor. Your secretary was astute there.'

'She was acting upon experience of her own,' said Bertram. 'She's divorced. I don't know the details.'

'Hm. Well, if the thing really has broken down it's no use struggling on,' said Mr. Manners. 'Much better cut the losses and end it. All other human partnerships are dissoluble, after all.' He sipped his brandy, meditating. 'She'll be pressed for money. That will be the immediate problem. We'll apply for legal aid, of course. That will take about a month to come through. We can either file a divorce petition at once or go to the magistrates for a maintenance order. If she can manage to wait and press for a divorce it will be better in the end.'

'You mean she'll be solely dependent on her own earnings for some time?'

'Yes, unless the husband voluntarily pays something, which seems unlikely in the circumstances. It's difficult enough to make them pay when there's a court order in force,' said Mr. Manners. 'The National Assistance people will help.'

'We can tide her over for a while,' said Bertram. 'She's a woman worth helping. We have a fund for emergencies like this.' He knew that aid to Marjorie now would mean unending loyalty from her in the future.

'Well, send her to my office tomorrow, Mr. Bliss,' said Mr. Manners. 'I'll have a talk with her and see what seems best. I'll probably hand her on to my partner, who deals with most of our divorce cases. He's a youngish man who's grown up with this developing situation. I do mostly conveyancing and probate myself.' He took a small diary from his pocket and consulted it. 'Three o'clock tomorrow would be a convenient time for me,' he said.

'Very well.' Bertram made a note in his own diary, which bore his initials defiantly on the front cover.

'Let me get you another brandy,' said Mr. Manners.

Sally had gone to the film of *Dr. Zhivago* with Wendy. Afterwards they went back to Wendy's room for coffee. She lodged in a tall old house in Warren End, not far from where Sally lived. Her landlady was a fierce widow with wispy grey hair and three cats; she watched over the morals of her lodgers relentlessly, eager to miss no excuse for suspicion. Now she peered out to make sure that it was not a licentious male accompanying Wendy into her premises so late.

'Nosy old bitch,' said Wendy, putting her thumb to her nose over the banisters as the landlady's door closed. 'I think she longs to catch me in compromising circumstances, just for the kick.'

They hurried up to the second floor, where Wendy had a room with a gas ring and a washbasin. One wall was bedecked with vivid travel posters, and a bright hand-woven spread covered the low divan. Sally took a cushion from it and sat down on the floor in front of the gas fire.

'In the end, they were parted,' she said, looking into the flames and seeing there Yury and Lara. 'He loved both of them, didn't he?'

Wendy looked consideringly at the kettle she had just filled. Then she unplugged it and went to the cupboard. She took out a bottle of Cinzano.

'You need something stronger than coffee,' she said.

'Oh, Wendy, how I've corrupted you!' Sally exclaimed. 'You never drank liquor till I led you astray.'

'Well, think what I missed in the years of my innocence,' Wendy said. *'Skol.'*

'It's awful about Mrs. Betts.' Sally switched her mind away from comparing the Zhivago triangle with her own. 'Poor little thing. She's so nice. Cowed, though. She's just the sort of person who's asking to be bullied, like those meek girls at school everyone got at.'

'She may not always have been like this,' said Wendy. 'That rotten man's probably knocked all the stuffing out of her.'

'Do you think she'll revive? Shall we witness a renaissance?' Sally asked.

'Who can tell? Old Babs'll see her right, anyway. That's for sure.'

'He's good in a crisis, I admit,' Sally said. 'Mrs. Seabright's turned up trumps too, hasn't she? People are surprising. Maybe she's not as hard-boiled as she seems.'

'Well, I expect she has a fellow-feeling for Mrs. Betts. It can't have been easy bringing those two boys up on her own. I like Tom.' Joan's two sons had often worked in the store during their holidays. 'Pity they're not a bit older,' Wendy went on. 'One for each of us.'

Sally did not rise to this. She drank the last of her Cinzano and looked at her watch.

'It's late. I must go, or Father will be ringing the hospitals,' she said.

'He doesn't really worry, if you're late, does he?'

'He pretends not to. He goes to bed and reads till I get home. I see his light go out under the door as I creep up the stairs,' Sally said. 'But I'm not often very late, not later than this. I have my gay life elsewhere.' She pulled a wry face.

'Oh, Sal, why don't you pack it in?' Wendy said. 'It's

103

wearing you out. Look at you, you're as thin as a wraith. You're destroying yourself.'

'I can't, Wendy. I simply exist until each time I see Derek. Nothing else counts.'

'But he'll never marry you, Sal. You say so yourself. You know he'll never be free.'

'He might, one day.' Sally turned an obstinate face to her friend. 'Angela might meet somebody else.'

'When she's got two small kids? Be your age.'

'It does happen. Or she might find out and leave him.'

'She'd make him give you up,' said Wendy.

'He wouldn't,' Sally insisted, clinging to this conviction without which she could not live. 'He couldn't.'

Wendy did not answer. She had never met Derek, and hoped that she never would. She condemned him unseen.

'If I knew my husband loved someone else, I'd leave him,' Sally said. 'Wouldn't you? Pride alone would make me. And I'd find someone else, just to show him.'

'I think I'd try to win him back, if I loved him,' Wendy said, trying to imagine it. 'I'd have all the claims, after all. The children, and the shared years.'

'The wronged wife. But I don't pity Angela,' said Sally, who could not bear to contemplate the other woman. 'He wouldn't have wanted me if he hadn't missed something from her.'

'He might just be bored,' Wendy suggested. 'An overdose of children and chores. You're different.'

'And if we ever did marry I'd go the same way, I suppose. Have children and get dull,' Sally said.

Derek was a lecturer in history at London University; he was clever and sensitive, liked Mozart and Monet, and was ten years older than Sally. These things Wendy had been told; he remained, to her, an enigma, and one she deplored.

'As long as he's in the world I'll never want anyone else,' Sally said.

'Well, I'm on the prowl,' said Wendy, feeling it time to leave this rarefied thinking. 'Honestly, what hope has any bright girl in this place? From Babs down to Paul, there isn't one real man in the store. They're all spineless, the lot of them. And a fat chance there is of finding anyone outside.'

'The town's full of men,' Sally protested. 'You've only to look out of the window. The pavements are smothered in them, walking about.'

'And have you looked at them closely?' Wendy demanded. 'What a bunch! They're spotted and pocked, or dirty, or both. And if you do find one who looks all right, how do you know what he'll turn out like ten years later? How do you know you're not shacking up with another Mr. Betts, may I ask? Or a Babs?'

'Maybe they turned out the way they have because of their wives,' said Sally. 'But probably not. Shirls is really a honey. I expect Betts would have bullied any woman, and is only drawn to potential victims. Someone else might not have stuck it so long. But you'll find a dishy fellow at the tennis club; wait until spring comes round again. Love will be lurking by the pavilion, you'll see, ready to be captivated by your backhand.'

Wendy flung a cushion at Sally. She was a good tennis player, and went to the club on the fringe of the town most nights in the season. Last year she had a brief romance with a young man who left in July to work in Accra. He had not written. Wendy had salvaged her self-esteem as best she could, saying it was all good experience, but she had been hurt.

When Sally at length got home she was surprised to see Bertram's car parked outside. What could Babs be doing here? She went round to the rear of the house. The kitchen door was not locked and she let herself in silently. Voices came from the study. She went quietly upstairs and into her bedroom.

A few minutes later, when Mr. Manners showed Bertram out, a light shone upstairs and the faint sound of a bath being run could be heard.

'Sally's back, I see,' Bertram remarked. 'Well, good night, Mr. Manners. Many thanks.'

He drove away, with a last glance at the illumined upstairs window in case, by some happy chance, Sally's form should be silhouetted against the thin curtain. But in vain. He thought of her there, naked, or wrapped in a towel; drying her body; powdering; brushing her short, red hair.

He went on up the road, through the town and over the bridge, then up Castle Hill, back to Shirley. She lay in their apricot bed, her hair in its plait, one large, bare arm flung up over her flushed, shining face, asleep.

13

Thursday was early closing day in Sedgemouth, and that afternoon Marjorie Betts set out with a list of rooms to let clipped from the local paper. She knew that if she and the children did not soon find somewhere else to live there would be an explosion in Joan's flat. Every evening, when the two women arrived back from the store, Michael and Amanda were already there. Joan had been obliged to get keys cut for each of them; there was no alternative, for their schools were not near one another, and they did not always get home at the same time. Amanda had Guides on Tuesdays, and Wednesday was games day for Michael. Both children did their best to remember that Joan's flat was not their own, but they came back hungry, and, in this weather, muddy; at once they made cocoa and spread thick slices of bread with butter and jam, as they had always done in The Grove. Joan had forgotten the capacity of schoolchildren for getting through food; her kitchen was perpetually crumby and tacky to the touch; she found sticky places on the chair where Amanda had dropped a blob of jam while eating as she read her history textbook. The children were not slatternly, but they were careless and unthinking, not used to such ordered surroundings. The house in The Grove was shabby and scuffed; one more mark on the scratched paint, one more stain on the frayed carpet, scarcely showed, and their mother had given up worrying about such trifles. But for Joan each evening now demanded a supreme effort not to scold or exclaim, and when ring marks from hot mugs placed straight on the wood appeared on her precious sofa-table she had to tell Marjorie that they must all move out soon.

'I know, I know!' Marjorie cried, and burst into tears, so that Joan felt a heel, but she did not weaken.

So now Marjorie was searching.

She wanted to sleep for a month. Her nerves were so taut that she jumped at the slightest sound. She was convinced that Peter would seek her out, if only for vengeance. Whenever Joan's telephone rang, which was frequently, she expected him to be the caller, having tracked her down in order to hurl obscenities at her. But so far he had made no move. Her hand was healing well. Mr. Manners had advised her, since the idea of reconciliation was clearly impossible, to file a plea for divorce on the grounds of cruelty. He had handed her on to his partner, a younger man who was kind in a brisk, impersonal way. No more could be done for the present; she must find a flat or a room, and struggle on, maintaining some hold on her own strength for if that went they were lost. This was all that there was.

She turned, newspaper cutting in hand, into a shabby

street of grimy terraced houses. The rain fell endlessly, yet children played in the road in front of the houses. A few ramshackle cars were parked by the kerb, and some long-haired louts in leather jackets were shouting angrily at one another. Without exploring the address in the advertisement she walked away.

Back at her flat, alone at last, Joan was cleaning up. She usually did her housework on Saturdays, but three days of invasion by the Betts family had left traces that must be expunged. She sighed over the white scorch marks on the table. The children had been properly appalled when their guilt was exposed, but they had not known how easily such things happen; the furniture at The Grove was all cheap, mass-produced stuff, mostly second-hand, and none of it merited cherishing. She polished hard and sighed again. Accidents like this no longer occurred in her well-ordered existence. Well, Marjorie would be sure to find somewhere to go during today's hunt, even if only temporarily, and she, Joan, could settle down again.

She had just finished wiping over the kitchen floor when the main door opened and Amanda came into the flat. School was over for the day. Her raincoat shone, soaked with rain from her journey; her satchel, which swung in one hand, dripped.

'Back already, dear?' Joan made her voice sound welcoming, yet calm. 'Put your damp things in the bathroom.'

The bathroom was already festooned with shabby underwear, hung to dry on strings over the bath. Thick woollen socks were spread on the towel rail. It was years since Joan had coped with such day-to-day problems; now, when Tom and Roger came back from college, she sent their things to the laundry.

Amanda obediently went into the bathroom. She put her rubber boots in a corner, and hung her raincoat over the towel rail beside Michael's socks; drips fell on the floor. Then she washed. She made a ceremony of it, filling the basin and leaning over it, and tears fell down her face into the water. She knew that Mrs. Seabright did not want them there, though she meant to be kind. They had tried to be tidy and good, but it was difficult when everything in the place was so precious; they were afraid now to touch anything. The carpets were pale; the chair covers felt like silk. She urged upon Mike the need for care, but how could a boy of ten be expected to live in a museum? He had got up early this morning to wash Mrs. Seabright's car before breakfast, as a gesture of gratitude, but when she discovered he had carried a bucket of soapy water through the flat, sploshing some on the floor, she'd tempered her thanks. Poor Mike. He'd gone up and down in the lift with his load. And it had rained all day since then, so what was the good? What was the good of anything?

Mum and Dad had finally broken up, that was certain. Amanda had often wondered how it would be when it happened. Many times at The Grove she'd lain in bed, listening, while Dad stormed round the house kicking the furniture and Mum cried. Then had come silence. Once, Amanda had crept to their parents' bedroom door; maybe Mum was dead, Dad might have killed her. She heard creaks, squeaks, and curious moans. Frightened, she went back to bed and hid under the sheets, where she lay trembling until, near morning, she slept. Next day Mum was not dead. She looked pale and heavy-eyed, but then she always did. Dad was red-faced and cross; no different.

At last she came out of the bathroom. Mrs. Seabright had put the kettle on and made hot buttered toast.

'We won't wait for Mummy and Michael. We'll have our tea, Amanda,' she said.

Amanda gulped as she saw the water poured into the pot. She hated tea; Mrs. Seabright had forgotten. She supposed she could swallow a bit. The toast would be nice; there was cherry jam.

That Thursday afternoon, while Marjorie was room-hunting and Joan cleaned her flat, Shirley Bliss went down to Eileen's house to make sure all was well. A few letters and circulars lay on the hall floor. She piled them neatly on the small table that stood at the foot of the stairs. Then she went round the house lighting the gas fires in each room to take the chill off the place, for it felt damp.

Eileen's mother's room was large and awesome, as though the formidable old lady's spirit haunted it still. The big double bed, where she had given birth to Eileen and her brother who had been killed in the war, and no doubt conceived them too, filled up most of the space. Eileen ought to sell it, and blot out the past; it was spectral; the bedspread, of faded silk, and the pink taffeta quilt, had covered it for most of Eileen's life, for old Mrs. Westcott had held tenaciously to what was familiar, refusing all change. She would not even accept a new mattress, but had clung to her own lumpy bed and her only daughter. Now Eileen was free, for the first time in her life.

Her room was brighter, a contrast to the rest of the house. There were books, rows of them, mostly thrillers and romances with occasionally a volume of poetry; this was how Eileen had escaped. There were prints on the wall, Van Gogh's 'Sun Flowers' and a Canaletto. A white sheepskin rug was by the bed, where Eileen's feet would rest on it morning and night. Her curtains were sprigged yellow chintz, her bedspread was white. A sewing machine and a small transistor radio stood on a table near the window. Photographs of Eileen's dead brother stood on a mahogany chest of drawers. Shirley looked at them curiously. She had never known Jim. One photograph showed him shy and self-conscious, but proud, in his uniform, the stripes of a corporal sewn on his sleeve; in another he was with a second young man, the two of them standing in front of an army truck and laughing.

Beside Eileen's bed was a Bible. Shirley picked it up. It was old and worn, much read. An inscription on the fly-leaf revealed that it had been given to Eileen on her tenth birthday by her grandmother. Idly, Shirley turned the pages; she had not opened a Bible for years. There were several cards inside, prints of religious paintings and illuminated texts, and one photograph, yellow and faded; it was of the young man in the snapshot with Eileen's brother. Clear, candid eyes looked out of an unlined face, soft with the blurred contours of youth. Shirley turned it over. On the back was written : *To Eileen, all my love, Bill*. There was no date. Jim Westcott had died at Dunkirk; perhaps Bill had too. Poor Eileen; Shirley had known nothing of this. Carefully she put the photograph back.

She went downstairs and into the sitting-room. It was crammed with furniture. Often she had sat here, while old Mrs. Westcott tyrannised from her chair. Eileen's tolerance and patience had been saintly; her life away from the shop had been dictated entirely by the whims of her mother. At least at Bliss's she had had a measure of freedom and opportunity, and now it was not too late for her to find some sort of happiness. She'd begun already; she must be got out of this melancholy shrine. Old Mrs. Westcott's resistance to change was evident here in this room : the chairs wore cross-stitched antimacassars; a Landseer-like stag brooded over the hearth and a picture of the late Queen Mary stood on the upright piano. Eileen must banish all this, or move; or both.

Shirley felt very depressed when she closed up the house again; it was a memorial, a morgue. She drove away in her red Mini thinking of the unknown young man with the wide, clear eyes.

Her most direct way home lay through the town. She decided to stop for tea at *The Copper Kettle*; it would cheer her up. Bertie was at a conference in the civic centre; shopkeepers and prominent citizens were meeting the town planners to discuss future development, each anxious to protect his own interests; so there was no need to hurry home.

Since it was early closing day, there was no parking problem and Shirley found a space outside the café. She sat at a small oak table on a spindly-legged chair, and ordered tea and a toasted bun. It was a typical English tea-room, with floral-overalled genteel waitresses and home-made preserves. A copper bowl of chrysanthemums stood in a niche, lit from below, and so badly arranged that Shirley longed to snatch the flowers out and do them again. Tweeded and mackintoshed ladies sat drinking their tea and talking. The air was faintly steamy as their garments yielded up some of the rain they had earlier absorbed. On ordinary days trade was brisk and tables hard to secure, but on Thursday afternoons most of the customers were cinema-goers or truants from neighbouring offices.

'Why, Mrs. Bliss! Good afternoon,' said a voice.

Shirley started, brought back to the present abruptly. She had been in a dream, watching a mental film in which Jim Westcott and Bill, under a hail of bombs, played the roles of doomed soldiers. She looked up and saw Mr. Manners standing beside her.

'I startled you, I'm so sorry,' he said. 'May I join you?'

Before she could answer he sat down at her table.

'I've been in court all day, and I need more than a cup of office tea to revive me,' he said. He was large and bulky, too big for the ridiculous chair on which he now perched. 'They have wonderful home-made scones here. Are you having some?'

'I've ordered a bun,' said Shirley, and added, 'I shouldn't, I'm too fat as it is, but I love them.'

'Oh, one bun won't hurt,' he said comfortably.

The elderly waitress set down Shirley's tea, her bun and some jam, and Mr. Manners ordered his own.

'Have some of my tea while you wait,' said Shirley, who felt she could not begin unless he did. 'Do you take milk?'

She poured out his cup and her own, then passed him the sugar. He took three lumps.

'Do eat your bun. It'll get cold,' he said.

'Have half.' Shirley sliced it in two and slid her plate towards him.

'Done,' he said. 'You shall share my scones.'

They spread jam on their segments of bun and began to eat; the butter had melted into the dough and tasted delicious.

'You looked very thoughtful, Mrs. Bliss, when I interrupted you,' Mr. Manners said between mouthfuls. 'What brings you to town on closing day?'

Shirley explained her errand.

'Oh yes. Sally told me you were holding the fort in the store for Miss Westcott,' he said.

'It's great fun. I wish I could do it always,' Shirley said.

'Why don't you, then?'

'Bertie doesn't approve. He thinks it's not proper, because he's the chairman,' she said, without a twinge of guilt at making such an admission.

Mr. Manners had no time to reply to this before the waitress arrived with his tea and scones, and a plate of cakes which she set down on the table. She was coyly amused when she saw how they had already shared out their assets. When she had gone, with belated discretion Shirley changed the subject.

'How's Sally? She's so clever, she's wasted in Sedgemouth,' she said. Then she thought that this was not a felicitous remark either, and added, 'I'm sorry, I shouldn't have said that.'

'Why not? It's true. But she deems it her duty to look after me,' said Mr. Manners. 'I've been at fault, drifting along and letting her do it; I realise it now. I must urge her to go further afield. She should go to London; she's got friends there. Perhaps in the spring.'

'Bertie won't want her to go,' said Shirley. She spread jam on a scone. 'He'll give her more money and persuade her to stay.'

'Well, one day she'll get married, and then we'll all have to let her go,' said Mr. Manners.

'Yes.' Shirley thought of the slight, dark man she had seen with Sally in London. Her father obviously knew nothing of his existence. 'Some more tea?' she said.

Mr. Manners accepted a second cup, then offered Shirley a cake. She chose a meringue.

'This looks good,' he said, selecting a piece of iced coffee cake. Then he glanced at his watch. 'I must keep an eye on the time,' he explained. 'My car's in dock and I don't want to miss the bus. They're not very frequent out to Warren End.'

'Let me run you back,' Shirley said at once. 'Please. It's no trouble. Bertie's out at a meeting, he won't be worrying.'

Mr. Manners demurred, but she insisted so he gave in. He paid for their tea, and they went out to Shirley's car. She was a good driver, he discovered; she used her gears well and did not fling her passenger against the side of the car when cornering.

'It's nice out here,' she said as they went along. 'You're nearer the coast than we are. Do you go down to the sea much?'

'Not now. We did when my wife was alive. She loved swimming. Sally goes sailing sometimes, or rather she did, with young Jessamy, but I don't think she went at all this summer.'

'Oh, Paul. Yes,' said Shirley.

'A dull but worthy young man,' Mr. Manners pronounced. 'I expect he'll go far. I'm sure he's got his whole future mapped out, even to where he'll live when he's fifty and the number of children he'll have.'

Shirley snorted with laughter at this view of Paul.

'Bertie thinks he's wonderful,' she said. 'But he is dull, you're right. He's a perfect yes-man.'

'Well, I'm glad Sally seems to have chucked him,' said her father. 'She needs someone a bit more lively.'

'Of course, she's a bit limited here in Sedgemouth, I suppose,' Shirley said. There must be doctors and school-masters; professional men. There was no university. 'Bertie only came here because of the war,' she added.

Hugh Manners wondered where Bertram hailed from originally. Somewhere not very different from Sedge-mouth, for sure. He wished a better fate for Sally than a second Bertram Bliss, and such thoughts filled him with compassion for the lady who was married to the first. She, too, deserved more.

'Won't you come in, Mrs. Bliss?' he asked, when they reached his house. 'Do let me offer you a drink.'

'It's too early,' Shirley said.

'It won't be, soon, if you'll come and tell me what it's like selling dresses all day,' he said.

So she did. He directed her upstairs to the bathroom, of which by now she was in need after so much tea, and while she was upstairs she heard him moving about below. She powdered her face and smoothed her hair, but for once she seemed tidy and matt.

Mr. Manners was in the sitting-room. He had a decanter of sherry and glasses set out on a tray, and was adding some logs to the fire.

'Sally's out, it seems,' he said. 'She must have been here this afternoon, though.'

Evidence lay on a chair: a workbox, and pieces of emerald green fabric.

'What a lovely colour,' said Shirley. 'That will suit her, with her hair. Was your wife auburn-haired?'

'Yes, she was. Carrot-tops, she called it, but it was beautiful,' he said. 'Sally's like her.' He suddenly got up and went from the room, returning a few minutes later with a photograph album.

'There,' he said, and showed Shirley a photograph of a young woman holding a baby. Her hair was longer than Sally wore hers, and her full-skirted dress looked odd, but the features were Sally's.

'How strange,' Shirley said. 'I thought daughters usually favoured their fathers.'

'She's quite like me in character,' Hugh said. 'Poor girl.' He turned a page of the album, and there was Sally as a schoolgirl, with long skinny legs and a smile all teeth. Her mother appeared again, looking softer and plumper as time passed. It seemed to be Shirley's day for nostalgia, but she was fascinated by the past. There was a boy, too. She had not known there was a brother, and feared to ask about him lest he, too, were the victim of tragedy. But Hugh soon told her.

'John's in Canada,' he said. 'He's older than Sally, as you can see from these. He's an engineer. He's getting married in March. To a Canadian girl.'

'He's out there for good?'

'Yes. He's been away six years now. He came back when his mother died, that's the last time we saw him.'

'You've never been out to visit him?'

'No.' Hugh closed the album, wondering what had made him reveal his family history in this way. Apart from Sally and his secretary, he was unused, now, to feminine company and it was surprisingly pleasant to be with a nice, kindly woman who was of a sympathetic disposition.

'You're going to the wedding, of course,' said Shirley.

'I haven't decided. I hope Sally will.'

'You must both go. It would be wonderful for you,' said Shirley. 'Whereabouts in Canada?'

'Vancouver. It's a beautiful place, with a much better climate than most of the country. Wonderful scenery, so close to the Rockies.'

'You must go,' Shirley repeated. 'You must meet your daughter-in-law. If you don't go, Sally won't either.'

She felt obscurely that both of them might have their lives transformed if they took this trip. Sally might forget her dark-haired lover, and Mr. Manners would find the interest of the journey stimulating. It crossed her mind to wonder if money was the trouble, but it could not be; Mr. Manners must do well as the senior partner in his firm, and Sally's salary was high.

'You're right, of course,' he said. He had not thought of that. His own hesitation was due chiefly to laziness; it would all be such an effort, like most things now. 'Now it's not too early for some sherry,' he said, and poured some into two glasses. 'Tell me about selling clothes to cross old ladies and teenage monsters with knees.'

She did, and he laughed at her jokes. With success, she grew bold, and confided how she felt timid among all the youthful assistants. She told of her awe of Mrs. Seabright and how it had fled.

Hugh found her humility disarming.

'I expect the youngsters, not to mention Mrs. Seabright, are much more scared of you than you are of them,' he said.

'Oh, no !' Such an idea had never occurred to Shirley. 'But I'm not frightening !'

She looked so dismayed at this notion that Hugh hastened to reassure her.

'No, but the young fear authority sometimes, if they don't despise it,' he said. 'It's your position I mean, not you. As a matter of fact, I rather think from what Sally tells me that you're top of the popularity poll in the store. What I meant was, you shouldn't be nervous.'

'You can't really tell what people think, can you?' Shirley said ingenuously. 'Unless they say.'

'No, often you can't,' he agreed. 'We're like icebergs, with only a bit on the surface for show.'

'And different bits for different people,' she said. She thought, I'm a totally different person in the store from when I'm at home with Bertie. And I'm different now. Bertie and I don't talk like this, ever.

That afternoon, Sally had been for a long walk in the rain, and at the end of it she telephoned Derek from a call-box. He stayed late at the college on Thursday and was accessible, removed from his family. By using a call-box, Sally avoided hiding from her father, whom she hated to deceive. When she got back to the house he was sitting by the fire smoking his pipe and looking at an old photograph album. As far as she knew, he had not opened it since her mother died.

'Ah, Sally,' he said when she came in. 'I'm playing golf on Saturday if the weather improves. I've just fixed a round with old Vernon.'

Sally stared.

'Oh, good,' she said, recovering herself. 'Let's hope the rain keeps off.'

'I met Mrs. Bliss in the town. She brought me home. What a nice soul she is.'

'She's a lamb,' Sally agreed. 'But a doomed one, I'm afraid.'

14

Hermione Tipps sat in the washroom and wept. Down her smooth, plump cheeks coursed a river of tears mixed with make-up; black streaks of mascara and eye-liner mingled with green from her lids.

'He's not worth it, love. None of them are,' said a voice.

'How do you know it's a fellow?' Hermione sobbed. However, she paused for a second, amid gulps.

'What else could it be?' Mildred Smith from Toiletries put her hand on Hermione's shoulder and gave her a bracing thump. 'Not in trouble, are you?' she asked more intently, looking closer at Hermione.

'No!' Hermione, shocked, ceased her wails.

'Then whatever's the matter?'

'He's given me the push, that's what,' Hermione said.

'Don't waste your strength on tears,' Mildred advised. 'Plenty more chaps about. Here, blow your nose.' She took a paper towel from a pile by the basins and gave it to Hermione, who obediently blew. For a whole week Paul had taken her out every night, either to the cinema, or driving, or to dinner; then he'd brought her back home and kissed her with seeming affection. Her mother had started to look at wedding-dress patterns; her father had talked about mortgage rates. Then, with no explanation, he'd dropped her flat; they'd had no quarrel. She still caught the early bus, but Paul avoided her on it, going upstairs; from the stop, he walked once more with Mr. Thomas. When they met in the store, and she made sure that happened, he nodded curtly and strode swiftly by, leaving her staring, biting her nails.

All this she now related to Mildred, choking a little but sobbing no more.

'That Jessamy, he's a proper old woman,' said Mildred bluntly. 'You're well rid of him. I was in Lighting for ages, I ought to know. He's after Sally Manners. Mr. Big-Shot, thinks no one else is good enough, but she won't give him the time of day. Good for her.'

Was that it? Slowly, painfully, light dawned. Hermione thought of her parents. Her mother, patient, tired, humble, had worked as a cleaner for years; her father was with British Railways, dealing with the parcels at Sedgemouth station. It wasn't like owning a pub; not that The

Swan at Birdsea was really a pub; it was grander, more a hotel. Mum had always been ambitious for Hermione; she'd had her taught dancing and elocution; then, when she'd left school, insisted that she went to the Tech. to learn typing. So she'd got her good job at Bliss's. She was learning shorthand now, though she'd skipped classes last week to go out with Paul.

'Give me another of them things,' she said, letting her carefully learned speech slip.

Mildred gave her another paper towel. She wiped the rest of her make-up off and stood up.

'I'll show him who's good for what,' she promised, running water into a basin. She began to wash vigorously, splashing her face and her eyes.

'That's right,' Mildred approved. 'Here, try my new Warm-Glo pancake.' She opened her handbag and took out a compact. 'We've some lovely new stuff on the stand, several novelty colours for eyes, and that. Come down and see.'

'I will do,' Hermione said. 'Thanks, Mildred.'

'Better now, then? Honestly, unless you fall for a baby, no man's worth a tear,' Mildred said.

'Maybe you're right,' Hermione said. 'I'll not be so silly again.'

'Bye-bye, then.'

Mildred left the washroom, swinging her hips in her green working dress. Hermione worked at her face, spreading on a thick mask that covered the traces of woe; she painted her lips silvery-white and blacked her lashes and eyelids. When all this was done, she too left the room, and met Mr. Bliss outside in the passage. He smiled at her as she flattened herself against the wall to allow him to pass.

'Carry on, Hermione my dear, carry on,' he said genially. 'How pretty you look today.'

She felt better. Old Babs was deceived; he'd detected

no sign of her grief. She'd wear her heart on her sleeve no longer; Mildred was right.

Bertram was happy today, for this weekend Eileen Westcott was due back from her cruise, and Shirley's escapade would be concluded. He hummed merrily under his breath as he went on his rounds. Postcards had come from Las Palmas and Malaga, gaudy and bright. She was having a wonderful time. She'd return ready for work and all that nonsense of Shirley's would come to an end; she'd settle down again quietly on the Hill, emerging suitably to attend her flower classes and her Townswomen's Guild meetings.

He sailed down in the lift to the basement. Things were better here now; Mrs. Betts was calming down. She'd found rooms in a house in Old Town; he supposed that this was satisfactory, though it gave her a long daily journey, and the children too. It would do for a time, at least. He'd had an unpleasant interview with the husband, a bellicose man who'd burst into the office demanding to see him. It seemed he'd searched for Marjorie first, but Paul had seen, or rather heard, his approach, for he'd shouted all the way down the stairs and through the department. With great presence of mind Paul had concealed Marjorie in his small office; Peter Betts had then literally gone to the top.

But Bertram was equal to most things; he'd been dealing with men all his life, though few he met nowadays were like Peter; however, there had been plenty of blustering loud-mouths in the army. Bertram had given him short shrift; he'd threatened to call the police and have him charged with making a nuisance and with insulting behaviour. Betts had soon gone. They'd not hear from him again.

Joan was restored, too, to her normal poise. She'd been severely disturbed by the presence of Marjorie, Michael and Amanda in her flat. Now they could all settle down.

Later on, he'd see what could be done about bringing Mrs. Betts upstairs to the office; Joan was right in suggesting that it would be a good plan. Her ideas were usually excellent and it was time he clarified her position. He meant to give her the title of executive aide, but this would mean taking her away from his personal mail. Still, if she and Marjorie could work in together, a system would evolve; luckily no open war had broken out between them while they lived together.

Mrs. Betts looked extremely tired and strained, Bertram decided as he watched her amid her lamps, competently attending to a difficult customer. When she had completed her sale, he told her he would drive her home that evening if she waited for him at the car.

Marjorie began to protest, but what was the point? She might as well accept any help that was going; goodness knows, she needed it. Accordingly, soon after half past five, she stood in the yard at the rear of the store in the drizzling rain, waiting for him to appear. She expected Mrs. Bliss to be present as well, but here she was wrong. Shirley's one concession to privilege was to arrive each morning at half past nine; she travelled in daily in her own car.

Bertram came into sight. He walked briskly, a small, important figure in his thick tweed coat and homburg hat.

'You should have got into the car, Mrs. Betts,' he chided, opening the door.

Marjorie had not liked to presume. But now she stepped into the Rover and relaxed, her mind an exhausted blank while Bertram drove out to Old Town.

When they reached her address he said, 'I want to see how you're placed, Mrs. Betts. Will you take me inside?'

She looked dismayed.

'Of course, Mr. Bliss, if you wish. But it's not quite what you're used to,' she said.

'Now, how can you know that, Mrs. Betts? I've

travelled the world in my youth,' said Bertram, as though Old Town and a tent at El Alamein were all one. He leaned across and opened the door.

She got out of the car. The house was a tall red brick semi-detached villa in an area that had seen better days. A dark, dripping laurel hedge hid the lower front rooms from passers-by. Dingy net curtains covered the windows. The front door was surrounded by panels of stained glass shaped geometrically; it was reached by a weedy path and opened into a square hall. Marjorie turned on the light and a feeble glow from a single bulb set high in the ceiling illumined the dull tiled floor and a square oak table.

'It works on a time switch,' Marjorie said. 'It goes out before you can get to the top.'

A smell of old, cooked vegetables filled the air, mingled with other less easily identified odours. Bertram's sensitive nose twitched; he distinguished wet wool, tobacco and cat.

Marjorie led the way upstairs. The staircase was wide and might have been elegant once; now the treads were covered in worn linoleum and the banister rail was scratched and splintery. Various sounds came from behind closed doors as they passed, climbing upwards; a piano gave out, over and over again, the opening bars of Beethoven's *Minuet in G,* carrying Bertram back to his youth and his mother with her metronome and conducting pencil. A typewriter clattered, a cat mewed, and as they approached the top floor, a wireless blared forth pop music *fortissimo*.

'Is the whole house let out?' Bertram asked.

'Yes. There are some students from the technical college and a journalist, and an Indian doctor who's learning the piano,' Marjorie said. The light went out, and she pressed a switch on the wall by the staircase which turned it on again.

She went on, and as the light went out for the second

time they reached the top floor. This was the source of the pop music, and as she opened a door the sound assaulted their ears with the raucous cacophony of too many decibels. Marjorie went straight to the transistor radio which stood on the table and turned it off.

'Oh, Mum, no!' came a wail, and immediately the noise resumed as the set was switched on again.

Marjorie snapped it off.

'Can't you see we've a guest?' she said angrily.

The children had not looked up when the door opened. They were sprawled at either end of a small settee which leaked stuffing from several large rents. Amanda's arm had stretched out to the radio, but she had not lifted her head from the book on her knee. On the small table in the middle of the room stood a half-full bottle of milk, a jar of jam and some butter still in its paper. A camp-bed filled one wall of the room; it was neatly made up, but laden with coats, books and some toys in an untidy heap. The roof sloped away to the window, and a gap in the wall led to an alcove that must once have been simply for storage; it held now a sagging double bed. On it lay a small, scruffy teddy bear.

The room was warm. A gas fire spluttered and popped.

'Is this all the space you have?' Bertram asked.

'Yes. Amanda and I sleep there,' Marjorie nodded to the double bed. 'Michael sleeps on the camp-bed.'

'Where do you wash? And cook?'

'There's a gas ring.' She pointed to one on the hearth. 'The bathroom's downstairs. There's only one in the house.'

Bertram was speechless.

'We manage,' Marjorie said. 'Everything else I saw cost too much.'

'What are you paying?'

'Three pounds a week. It's cheap, really, for two rooms,' Marjorie said.

The space could hardly be described as two rooms, Bertram thought.

'We can never go to the toilet,' Michael said. 'It's always engaged.'

Amanda glared at him.

'We'll find something better soon,' Marjorie said. 'This will do for now.'

Mr. Bliss was still taking in details. He saw packets of sugar and tea on the mantelpiece; three eggs on a plate; a piece of cheese and a packet of cornflakes.

'What are you going to have to eat this evening?' he asked. He supposed they had a sort of high tea.

'We'll pop down to the shop on the corner for some fish and chips,' Marjorie said in a bright voice. 'That will be nice, won't it, children?'

'Yes, Mum,' said Amanda. Her voice was lifeless. Bertram peered at her in the dim lighting. Her hair was limp and her school tunic had spots on the front; her face was white apart from an angry red pimple on her chin; she looked ill and unhappy.

Michael said, in a whine, 'When can we go home? I don't like it here,' and Amanda kicked him hard on the shin. He at once began to sob loudly.

Marjorie looked as if she would soon be in tears too, and Bertram was not surprised. He took out his wallet and withdrew a five-pound note. Above the tumult, he spoke.

'Take the children out to supper tonight. Use the rest of the money over the weekend. Go for a trip to the country; get out of here. And come and see me at ten o'clock on Monday. You can't stay here. We must make other arrangements.'

He turned away then, and left her to console her weeping offspring, hurrying downstairs, past the typewriter, the cat, and the piano which now resounded with vigorous, inaccurate arpeggios. When he reached the hall he heard the pop music start up again.

Bertram hastened back to Castle Hill, for once ignoring the speed limit as he sped back to cleanliness and comfort.

After dinner that night he took out his stamps and began to select some items for barter with a corresponding philatelist in Finland. It was peaceful in the large, pleasant room. Shirley, dressed in a long tweed skirt and a frilled chiffon blouse, reposed on the sofa, her shoes off and her feet hidden under the folds of thick fabric she wore. She was watching a play on television; sinister men plotted blackmail in a yacht at Amsterdam.

Bertram said, holding a stamp to the light to inspect it, 'I'm not happy about Mrs. Betts. She's in unsuitable rooms in Old Town. I think she'll collapse if she stays there. Then the children will be taken into care by the authorities and we'll have a difficult job to get them out and her back to normal.' He described to Shirley the scene he had witnessed. 'The children don't understand what's happened, at least the boy doesn't. I think the girl does; she's older. I doubt if their mother has been able to explain it to them. They don't look well. I don't think they can even get to the lavatory.' He repeated Michael's remark.

'But what else can she afford?' Shirley asked. 'I don't suppose that room was meant for a family. It's probably intended to be let to a single person, or a working couple.'

'If the children were older they might co-operate more,' Bertram said. 'At least these two seem to be obedient; they come straight back from school.'

'They won't always,' said Shirley. 'If it's not nice at home they'll stop out. They'll meet other children, perhaps get into gangs. What can we do, Bertie? Can you pay her more?'

'Not officially. We'll have everyone wanting a rise if she gets one,' he said. 'She's already putting in longer hours than before. I want to promote her to help Joan, eventually, but at the moment she isn't capable of more. I can't do it just out of pity for the woman.'

'Oh dear,' said Shirley.

'I only hope Mrs. Betts has the spunk to pull out of this,' said Bertram. 'Look at how Joan's managed.'

'She told me her parents helped her,' said Shirley. 'And she's made of tougher stuff. What about Mrs. Betts's parents?'

'They're dead. And her only sister lives in Australia.'

'Poor soul. I suppose she has very little time to go looking for rooms,' said Shirley. 'I could try to find somewhere. I'll have plenty of time now. I might discover something.'

He had not had to suggest it; she had volunteered.

15

Eileen returned full of traveller's tales. She was tanned, and had put on weight. The cruise had been a success. She produced a leather pochette, thonged and ornamented, as a gift for Shirley.

'I don't know what you'll use it for,' she said. 'But I thought it was pretty.'

'I'll put mending wool and cotton reels in it,' said Shirley. 'Thank you.'

She had brought bread, milk and eggs for Eileen, and now urged her to come up to Castle Hill for dinner, for the little house seemed to her to be desolate, despite the lighted fire and the flowers she had arranged. But Eileen refused, saying she had a lot to do before starting work again.

Despite entreaties, she insisted, and Shirley left, defeated. She felt somewhat forlorn as she returned home.

Eileen seemed withdrawn, as if her foreign experience had lifted her away from her former life. Though eager to describe all she had seen and done, she was preoccupied and intent upon proving her self-sufficiency. Still, in the morning, she would be pleased to see Shirley in the store for an hour or two while she learned what had happened in her absence.

But when Shirley arrived in the fashion department the next day, Eileen was busy in her office checking lists with Maud, and seemed astonished to see her.

'Didn't you expect me?' Shirley tried to conceal the dismay she felt at Eileen's swiftly concealed look of impatient surprise. 'I thought there might be some loose ends to tie up,' she added defensively.

'Everything seems in perfect order,' said Eileen, recovering herself. 'Maud's just been bringing me up to date. You've done very well.'

It was true. The sales figures for the past fortnight were better than for the same period the year before, and Eileen had been made uneasily aware that she was not indispensable; Shirley's action in filling the breach had not had altogether the result she wanted.

'I see.' Shirley looked about. All was perfect. Her efforts had not been needed; perhaps behind her back she had been mocked for making them. She left at once, walking off through the gowns and the coats, looking neither to the right nor to the left. The next thing was to hunt for rooms for the Betts family; that, at least, was urgent work.

With her mind fixed on this purpose, Shirley went straight to the offices of the nearest house agents; here, she spent some time in consultation, and emerged with lowered spirits and a list of addresses to view. By the time she had been to see the available rooms she felt thoroughly depressed, and understood why Marjorie had been obliged to settle for such unsuitable accommodation in

Old Town. She saw rooms with peeling wallpaper and chipped sinks; rooms with pipes carrying plumbing that creaked overhead, and bare, wooden floors; rooms with broken furniture and strange lingering smells. It was soon very clear that for what she could pay, Marjorie and her children would be inadequately housed. Shirley went home at last with the odours of stale sweat, old kipper and general stuffiness in her nose.

She had a bath, to wash it all away, and lay in the warm scented water, brooding, with her pale, heavy body stretched out. First she worried about Marjorie Betts and the children. Then her thoughts moved on to Eileen. People did not need one's pity, nor even one's aid, for long; any vague ideas Shirley had of popping in from time to time to help out must be banished. Empty weeks stretched ahead. She lay in the water and tried to think of something that might be anticipated with pleasure. Christmas would soon be here; it could be regarded more as a diversion from monotony than in any other light. It would mean a visit to Bertram's mother on one of the days; the old lady would never come to stay with them, preferring, she said, her own bed. In fact, she had many friends in the village where she lived and would not surrender her gay life to one of boring luxury in Cedar Grange.

There would be Christmas dinner with neighbours on the Hill, who would return to the Blisses' on another night for a meticulous return of hospitality. Then it would be over, a brief burst of spurious gaiety. After that, months of winter would stretch ahead, long, cold, and lonely.

Shirley, lying in the bath, wept for herself; she wept for her lost youth, and her lost illusions, and her lack of hope. After a little while she recovered enough to scold herself, for had she not almost everything a woman could want? She had a good husband whom she unquestioningly loved, a fine home and plenty of money. It was ungrateful to wish for more. She gave up at last and got out of the water.

She dried her soft white body, and sprinkled it well with talc. Then she dressed, in a long green skirt and a golden sweater, to await the return of Bertie.

He came in, rubbing his hands, looking brisk and pleased with himself. He bent to kiss her forehead as she sat on the sofa, with her face lifted to receive the ritual salute. She knew, at the touch of his lips, that the gesture was a habit as deeply ingrained as the nightly brushing of his teeth.

He said, 'Well, dear, here's some news to please you. Your flower ladies are holding a display in aid of some charity or other, and want us to provide a fashion show as an added attraction.' He took a letter from his pocket and gave it to her.

Shirley frowned as she read it. She really needed glasses. The exhibition was to be at Moreton Priory in March.

'Of course we'll oblige,' said Bertram.

'I should think so. It will be a good advertisement,' said Shirley. She handed the letter back. Lady Murcott, the president of the group, had written direct to Bertie; she, Shirley, a leading member, had not been asked to arrange the matter. Of course, she had seldom been at home in the past weeks, she reminded herself, and had missed the last meeting, but she had sold Lady Murcott a suit only last week. Why had she not mentioned the idea then?

'Our fashions will draw a larger audience than your flowers,' said Bertie. 'Eileen is very pleased. She's going to show an expensive collection; people who go to such things have money to burn. We might make quite a good thing out of it.' Still smugly smiling, he went off to wash.

After dinner, they sat as usual in their living-room, Shirley on the sofa with a book she was not reading, and Bertram at his desk, bent over his stamps.

She said at last, 'Bertie, I looked at rooms for the Betts, but I couldn't find anything suitable at such a low rent.'

'Not to worry, my dear,' said Bertram. He opened his

African section. The politics of these countries were so fluid and their names so altered that correct cataloguing must be meticulous. 'Eileen is taking them in. She agreed at once when I suggested it. She thinks the house will be too large for her now, on her own. It's an excellent solution.'

Shirley said, stupidly, 'You asked me to find somewhere.'

'You offered, my dear. I didn't request it,' said Bertram smoothly. No need to remember that he had intended her to do so, and no need either to reveal that Joan, who felt guilty about the plight of the Betts, had come up with this idea. Eileen, summoned, had consented doubtfully to a trial period.

So in this, too, Shirley had not been needed.

At Warren End that evening, Sally and her father had begun a game of Scrabble, which they each played because they thought the other enjoyed it; once, it had been a genuine craze.

'You'll go to John's wedding, won't you, Daddy?' Sally asked, setting out OXEN at right angles to Hugh's CRAVEN.

'Why don't we both go?'

'Well, maybe.' Sally would not commit herself yet. How could she voluntarily separate herself and Derek by six thousand miles? 'I might be able to get away,' she said.

'Nonsense, dear. You could go at any time.'

Last April, she had met Derek. They had emerged from the Doge's Palace in the same group of sightseers. She had said to her companion, a woman encountered on the plane flying out, 'I feel sated with primary colours. Oh for some green.' Derek had overheard the remark and grinned. Later, at dinner in the ship setting off for Piraeus, he had picked up this remark of hers and they had held a long conversation about Renaissance art and the Impressionists. A long time afterwards he had told her that she had won his heart by daring to admit that one could see too many blue-robed Madonnas trimmed with gold.

'Bliss eats out of your hand,' said her father. 'You can do what you like.' He laid T, A and I around his daughter's X, collecting a triple score.

Sally knew that she could take her leave whenever she liked, but she had a foolish hope that Derek might have to depart on some sort of research to a distant land where she might, by chance, be loitering. He had gone to Greece to tread in the steps of Aeschylus. At the last moment Angela's mother had broken her leg, so that he went alone. It had begun as simply and tritely as that. Now, even their future meetings were jeopardised. Derek had a friend who was often away on country visits at weekends. He never minded Derek using his flat, and asked no questions; Sally wondered if, in fact, he knew the truth. When Derek left her there alone, late at night, as he often did to hurry back to his wife and children, she wondered what would happen if the friend came back too soon and found her. Derek's wife seemed to accept that he must sometimes be late or away; he was researching for a book, and an excuse of reading seemed to satisfy her; Sally did not ask what tale was told, for some things were better not discussed. But now all this was threatened: Derek's friend was to marry and the flat would no longer be available; they must make other plans.

'We'll think of something,' Derek said.

'Is it true? It's not an excuse? It's not that you want to stop and won't tell me?' she had agonised.

'I'll never give you up,' Derek insisted.

You will one day, she shrieked inside. One day you'll be tired of all the deception and the subterfuge. It simply won't be worth the trouble. But she could not bear to contemplate this, just as she could not bear to think of Derek's wife.

The crossword grew slowly. Hugh knew that his daughter was not always happy. He had no idea of the cause, and so he saw no way to help her, but he realised now, in some shame, that she should feel herself free.

He said, 'We could hire a car and drive through the Rockies. I'd like to see Lake Louise. Or we could go to San Francisco. It might be too early in the year for the mountains. It would be fun.'

'Yes, it would.' Two or three weeks were not long to be away. If she did not go, her father might find some excuse too, or might return straight after the wedding. There were times when she did not see Derek for several weeks, but he always wrote or telephoned so that they were in contact. Thus she existed, from one islanded instant to the next. Voluntarily to make communication more difficult was against every instinct.

She laid ACQUIT on the board, getting rid of the Q at last.

Whilst Sally and her father played Scrabble, down in Old Town Marjorie Betts was frantic. She had arrived back at ten to six full of the news of their impending move, to find neither of the children in the room. It was dark and cold; the veneer of order she had managed to impose after breakfast was undisturbed. They had clearly not returned.

Perhaps the Indian doctor two floors down had waylaid them and was giving them tea.

Perhaps the journalist had found them unable to open the door, and taken them in.

She hurried down and knocked on each door in turn. The journalist, who was annoyed at the interruption, had seen nothing of the children and had, indeed, been enjoying freedom from the pop music which played incessantly after their return. He shut his door firmly upon her and hastened back to his typewriter.

The Indian couple showed more concern. They shook

their heads and frowned in sympathy. No one else in the house had seen the children.

Marjorie sat on the stairs and wondered what to do. She tried to reason calmly. They came back from school separately, so that if one had met with an accident, the other should be here. But one, arriving home and finding the other absent, might have panicked and rushed off to search, then got lost.

There was a public telephone for the use of tenants in the hall. She rang the schools in turn. There was no reply from either. At this time of night, they were, of course, locked and deserted. She was about to ring the hospital when the Indian doctor came pattering down the stairs in his carpet slippers.

'Mrs. Betts, please. I think we should ring the police,' he said.

16

At first the children were excited, going back to their old house. Amanda was pleased to see her own room again, though it was bare and had none of her toys or clothes left in it. But the pictures of horses still hung on the wall, and her white-painted bed was still there. It felt strange, though, without their mother. And everything was so dirty; dust was on every surface; there were unwashed plates in the sink and a curious, musty smell in the air, quite different from the one at the house in Old Town.

Their father had collected them from school. When Amanda came out of hers, there he was, waiting outside in the car. She was pleased to see him, hugged him warmly, and hopped eagerly in to sit at his side. Faint fumes came from him; she did not know what caused them, but they were familiar, part of him, like his red face and wispy brown hair.

'We'll collect Michael, then we'll go home,' Peter Betts said.

Michael was already at the bus-stop, outside school, waiting in a scuffle of small scrubby boys for the Old Town bus to arrive.

'Where are we going?' he asked, clibing into the car.

'Why, home of course,' said Peter, driving off.

When they reached The Grove, there was no tea ready. There was half a stale sliced loaf, but no jam, and a few soggy biscuits in the larder. Amanda made cocoa with milk from an opened tin, and tea for the others. They ate and drank while their father talked heartily to them about their doings in a way he had never done before. Michael replied eagerly, but Amanda was silent.

'It's horrid where we live. Can we stay at home now?' Michael asked. He had found the remains of a packet of Sugar Puffs and was eating them with the last of the milk. They were damp and soft, but he liked them just the same.

'Well, we'll see,' said Peter cagily. He had acted on impulse, finding himself back in town before the schools closed. The children were his, weren't they? He'd as much of a right to them as their mother. Fostering the whim, he decided he mourned for them.

'Mum will wonder where we are,' said Amanda.

'Oh no, she won't. I arranged it with her,' said Peter airily.

Amanda subsided and drank her cocoa. Then she went to the sink and began to wash the accumulation of dishes and cutlery that were untidily stacked. Peter drank more tea, noisily: the family man, a poor misunderstood father revelling in the company of his children. He suppressed a belch. Then he got up and lurched from the room. The children heard him enter the lavatory and lock the door.

Amanda washed up in silence. She cleared the rest of the things from the table and did them too.

'Now get your homework out and do it, Michael,' she said.

Surprised, but docile, Michael obeyed. When their father came back into the room they were sitting at each side of the table intent on their books.

'What? Too busy to spare a word for your father after all this time?' Peter asked in tragic tones. 'Come on. No homework tonight. We're going to the pictures.'

Alone in the lavatory, he had realised that the evening stretched ahead, tedious unless filled. He had never really known how the children spent their time; they must, he supposed, be fed at some stage, as certainly must he. He'd give them sausages and chips in the Regal café, then they'd watch the film. They'd find him a jolly good chum.

'We must do our homework, Dad,' said Amanda.

'Oh, do it in the morning. Or leave it for once. I'll write to your teachers,' said Peter grandly. 'Come along, now. Put up your books.'

They were still in the cinema when the police called at The Grove. So the sergeant found the house dark and deserted. Shining his torch through the windows, he saw dust, and the tidy sink. It looked unoccupied. From where he stood, the children's satchels, laid on the floor, were out of sight.

Marjorie would not leave the house in Old Town in case there was news or the children came back. She was convinced now that Peter had abducted them; you read of such things. He wanted revenge, and might spirit them out of the country for all she knew, though she supposed that this would cost money and he usually drank all his.

136

She sat drinking cup after cup of tea, trying to stave off utter panic. Till midnight, the Indian doctor's gentle little wife kept her company, and was there when the police reported a blank at The Grove. Then, murmuring regret, she left, urging Marjorie at least to lie down and try to rest, but such a thing was impossible. Several times, Marjorie went down to the street, staring up the length of road, but no one came.

The film was good, a cowboy drama, and Michael enjoyed it. He sat forward in his seat, sucking an iced lolly, quite content. But Amanda fretted. In a way, it was nice to see Dad, yet she knew it was wrong somehow. They'd no pyjamas or washing things; Mum wouldn't have let them go off like that, without. Perhaps she was ill, or dead, and Dad wasn't telling. She began to plot.

They returned to the house and were told to go to bed. So thoroughly had Joan and Marjorie cleared their clothes that nothing was left behind.

'Sleep in your vests,' said Peter. 'Shirts too, if you like.' He went to the cupboard where he had a bottle; it was hours since he'd had a nip.

Michael was soon undressed and in bed.

'You must wash, Michael,' Amanda told him sternly. She put on her raincoat over her vest and went along to the bathroom. Somehow, here, it seemed important to up-hold her mother's standards, although she had often kicked against them before.

Michael had no intention of copying her example. He lay in bed and shivered; the sheets were cold and damp. It was nice being back in his room, with his football stars pinned to the wall.

Amanda came back with her teeth chattering. There was no hot water; the boiler was out. No wonder the house was cold. A small geyser supplied the kitchen sink. Their mother had always made up the boiler, morning and night. She got into her own bed and pulled the clothes up to her chin, willing sleep to stay away. She pinched herself and recited *The Wreck of the Hesperus* under her breath, then the capitals of Europe, but they acted as a lullaby and she almost dropped off. She got out of bed and walked up and down the room. It was icily cold, so she put on her clothes again. At last she dared to open her door and peer out.

The house was silent, and totally dark. She crept to the door of the room where her parents had slept, and listened. She heard snores and a grunt. So, he was asleep.

Amanda went quietly into Michael's room. He was sleeping, his mouth a little open, one arm across the pillow. She shook him gently, then put her hand over his mouth as he stirred.

'It's all right, Mike. It's only me. Keep quiet,' she ordered, shaking him harder while keeping his mouth muffled. 'We've got to escape,' she said, and began to explain.

'But why? I'm tired. Let's wait till tomorrow,' Michael said, retreating into his bed again.

'We can't wait. Dad's going to Hull tomorrow, he said so. He might decide to take us too. Then what should we do? We'd never know about Mum.'

'Oh, all right then.' Still very unwilling, Michael gave in. He got out of bed and dressed, grumbling and yawning.

Amanda kept urging him to keep quiet and hurry, until at last he was ready. Holding their breaths, they tiptoed down the stairs and into the hall. Softly, Amanda opened the front door.

Then she remembered their satchels. She sent Michael back for them, wondering whether to leave a note for their father. It would mean using a light, so she decided against the idea; so far, they had managed by feel, creeping down the familiar stairs with hands outstretched to ward off the known obstacles. The front door made a slight sound as it

closed, and they paused for a minute, but nothing happened. No light came on in the bedroom above.

They set off together, walking hand in hand, with their
satchels trailing and bumping against their legs. There
were few people about, for it was very late now, and rain-
ing. They saw no cars until they reached the main road,
then one or two went past, their tyres splashing water up
off the wet road. Aanda knew the way to the centre of
the town, over the bridge, and then out again to Old
Town, but not the more direct route, the single side of the
triangle. They had been walking for quite a long time
before a policeman saw them.

17

Sally hated dressing the windows in sales weeks. Making
out-of-date fashions and piles of sheets look alluring was
a chore.

'We'll cheer ourselves up with a ski window next week,'
she told Wendy, when they had spent hours changing the
Christmas displays for the annual bargains. 'And what
shall we do with these dear boys now, I wonder?' she went
on, surveying the row of Oriental Monarchs, now redun-
dant, stacked in the workroom.

'Let's decorate the Star ballroom with them for the
dance,' said Wendy. 'A frieze of kings.'

'Hm. Seems a pity to chuck them out. Maybe Babs will
want them stashed away. They could be used again when
enough years have passed for people to forget them, I
suppose.'

'They were a success,' Wendy said.

'Goodness knows what we'll be able to dream up next year,' said Sally. It seemed very far off.

'You'll come up with a notion,' said Wendy.

'Your confidence is touching,' Sally said. She looked at a bearded face. 'With a bit of touching up he could be Neptune,' she added. 'We could have mermaids, mermen and a treasure chest. We could bisect the rest of these chaps and give them fishtails.'

'I don't know how you think of these things,' said Wendy. 'They're a bit over-dressed, aren't they? I suppose we could cut off their robes.'

'Hairy chests and seashell necklaces,' said Sally. 'It's a thought.'

'How shall I deal with Paul at the dance?' Wendy said.

'What do you feel like?'

'Hard up I may be, but not desperate,' said Wendy. 'Are you sure you won't swop? I'd adore to have your father as my partner.'

'No fear,' said Sally. 'You stick to Paul. I must protect my parent.'

Wendy threw a dirty paint cloth at her, and she ducked as the door opened and Mr. Bliss came in. He picked up the rag and gave it to Wendy, and then wiped his hands on a spotless handkerchief. 'I came to congratulate you both on excellent displays during the Christmas period,' he said, ignoring the distraction. 'The best windows we've had, I'm sure. Well done.'

You had to hand it to Babs. He was never ruffled, and he did his stuff. Nothing one did went unappreciated.

'And now you must both be looking forward to the dance,' he told them emphatically. 'A well-deserved festival night.' He was standing close enough to Sally to see the faint, fine down on her cheek, and the trace of a tiny scar on her forehead. He could smell the perfume she used.

'Father is looking forward to it very much,' said Sally with truth. His dinner-jacket had been specially cleaned and he had promised to buy a new evening shirt; Sally advised one with trendy pleating.

'Good, good. Well, bring hearty appetites to Cedar Grange,' Bertram urged. 'My wife is planning quite a feast.'

She probably was. Shirley's repasts were famed.

He left at last. Sally pulled a face after him.

'He gets worse and worse. He's positively maudlin, drooling on,' she said disgustedly. 'Why do we stick it?'

'Poor old Babs. He has got it badly. I feel quite sorry for him,' said Wendy. 'Just as well I was here to be gooseberry. You wait, he'll be cutting everyone out so that he can dance cheek to cheek with you all night.'

'What do you bet?' Sally picked up a sheaf of sketches. 'Enough of this lewd talk. I must go and see Joan about the ads for next week's *Echo*. The coast will be clear up there now Babs has gone on his rounds.'

Wendy, left alone and with no pressing work to do, fell to musing. She had heard on the store grapevine about Hermione Tipps and her brief fling with Paul Jessamy, and felt bitter about the callous way in which she had been discarded. Hermione was extremely young, and not very experienced; she had been hurt. Wendy's own wound of the summer was recent enough to smart still when she thought of it. There must be kinder ways of ending things, ways in which pride, at least, was saved. But how? What could be done if all interest had fled? Hermione, it was true, was now cheerfully consoling herself with young Joe Phelps from Paul's own department; he was a much more appropriate companion for her, but it could be the defiant gesture of one on the rebound. Wendy decided that the night of the dance might be livened up if she made an opportunity to avenge Hermione.

Eileen Westcott would be escorted by Mr. Thomas to

that function. Annually they attended Cedar Grange to dine amid the assembled august company, then proceeded together to The Star, united for the journey in the back of Bertram's car, their knees covered by a mohair rug, with Mr. Thomas's prudently withdrawn towards the side of the car lest any slight misleading contact might occur as they rounded a bend. Mr. Thomas stayed only until eleven o'clock, dancing with Mrs. Bliss and Miss Westcott as was his duty, but with no one else. He held his partner warily at arm's length and marched her briskly round the perimeter of the floor, no matter what the tempo of the band. At the end of this fearsome ordeal, he flitted thankfully to refresh himself at the running bar, among the males.

After her cruise, Eileen had settled down quickly and taken in her stride the advent into her home of the Betts family. At first, she felt she had been bounced into consenting to take them in; Joan and her petition had caught her by surprise, giving her no time for prudent reflection. But in a very few days a whole new easy way of life had evolved that made her forget she had spent so many years solely at the beck and call of a querulous old lady. Gradually, they had arranged the house. Michael slept in the dining-room, which by day was the Betts' retreat, where homework, painting, radio playing and messy pastimes were pursued. Marjorie had old Mrs. Westcott's bedroom, and Amanda the small third bedroom above the hall.

In the evenings, after the children were in bed, Marjorie joined Eileen in the sitting-room. Queen Mary had been banished from the piano; the cross-stitch antimacassars had disappeared; a television set had been hired, and the children, by invitation, watched certain programmes. At weekends they all ate together as a family; slowly, the bastions were crumbling and the divisions becoming less pronounced. At Christmas an exhausting but riotous time had been spent by them all. Eileen was so used to caring for her mother that it seemed natural to help Marjorie. Under this thoughtful regard Marjorie began to relax, to laugh, to dare to look ahead. They shared the shopping and the chores, even the kitchen, so far in total harmony. In fact, Eileen thought it would be hard to quarrel with anyone as meek and self-effacing as Marjorie.

The children, after their confinement in Old Town, patently revelled in the space and freedom of their new home. They shouted and sang, and Marjorie kept apologising for their noise, saying she had never known them so boisterous. Eileen, once her ears became attuned, found that she enjoyed their happy shrieks; she was gratified when they rushed to tell her of their doings, and when they hugged her at bedtime. At Christmas they gave her gifts they had hastily made themselves, a knitted tea cosy from Amanda and an unidentifiable fretwork animal from Michael. They sang carols on Christmas Eve while Eileen played the old piano, a thing she had not done for years.

Their father was supposed to have them for the day on Boxing Day. After their disappearance this plan, reluctantly accepted by Marjorie, had been devised by the lawyers as a way to prevent further trouble. But Peter never turned up to claim them; they sat about in their best clothes, all morning, waiting. He did not come, and he sent no message.

The children were interested in the forthcoming Christmas dance at The Star Hotel. They grew quite excited discussing Eileen's plans about her clothes, and urged their mother to go to the dance too.

'Oh no. I couldn't,' said Marjorie.

'Why not?' Eileen thought it a good plan too.

Marjorie made a half-hearted excuse about the children being left alone, though in fact neither would have minded. They had spent so much time alone together as it was that they would never have given it a thought, and here they were surrounded by friendly neighbours. But Marjorie was nervous about leaving them at night; she still feared a hostile act by Peter.

As the days passed, she grew more certain that her right course was to carry on as best she could alone. The children's improved health and spirits confirmed her in this opinion, and her own progress; she slept better, and ate well. She found Eileen a calm pillar of support such as she had never known before, one who seemed to want to help her with her burdens. Whole days passed with never an unpleasant thing occurring; she developed a nightly habit of rehearsing in her mind all that had happened in the hours before, and counting up the good events to set against the bad. There was no question about which side won. Usually the worst thing that happened in a day now was a difficult customer, or a laddered stocking. How different from before.

She obscurely felt that this change in her fortunes was due to Bertram; he it was who had contrived that Eileen should offer them a home. He continued as their bene-factor, and often in the evening drove her and Eileen home, heedless of the detour it made for him. Amanda and Michael had by this time lost their awe of him; he teased them, slipped them an occasional half-crown, and seemed like a kindly uncle.

As the day of the dance drew nearer, the whole house-hold concentrated on getting Eileen ready to attend. It was Marjorie's Saturday at the store; she and Eileen now alternated so that there was someone at home each week-end to keep an eye on the children. This time, Michael set off to do the shopping, armed with a large basket, a neatly written list, and the black leather purse that held the housekeeping money, while Eileen went to the hair-dresser. She came back, mildly bouffant, to find that

Amanda had set the table and peeled the potatoes, and made a jelly. By the time Marjorie arrived home in the evening, they were all sitting round the television watching *Dr. Who*.

Eileen was to wear a splendid dress of green velvet. In it, she looked elegant; it gave shape to her rather dumpy figure, and concealed the flat-heeled pumps she wore for comfort.

'You look beautiful,' Amanda generously said.

Michael remained detached from this female interchange. He was sick of all this fuss about clothes. After all, it was just an old party. He was busy drawing a sailing dinghy like Paul Jessamy's *Mary Lou* on a block of paper he had been given for Christmas.

Just as Eileen was at last ready and had passed inspection, her nails coral pink and her eyelids faintly green, the telephone rang.

Bertram Bliss was the caller. He said that Sally Manners could not now come to dinner; it left them a lady short, and would Marjorie please take her place?

'I've nothing to wear!' Marjorie was aghast. A word from Bertram was to her in the nature of a royal command, and must, if humanly possible, be obeyed.

'We'll find something.' Eileen's hand covered the telephone so that Bertram could not hear their discussion. His voice came squeaking through the receiver and she hurriedly put it to her ear again. 'What did you say? I'm sorry?'

Bertram impatiently repeated that Mrs. Phillips would come down and stay with the children immediately after she had washed up following the dinner-party, in a taxi paid for by himself.

'Oh, how thoughtful!' More than ever, Marjorie must carry out Mr. Bliss's wishes.

She had, in truth, no smart dress of her own. With Peter, there had been neither the money to buy, nor the occasion to wear one. But Eileen had several; she was not a fashion buyer for nothing. Marjorie was slighter, and a little taller; she did not fill out the copper sheath that Eileen had bought for her holiday, and whose darts they now hastily took in with tacking stitches, but it did not swamp her, and its length, a little long on Eileen by contemporary standards, was modishly short on Marjorie and displayed her slender legs.

'Mum, you look fab,' said Michael.

'I wish I'd had my hair done,' Marjorie lamented, but she was quite excited. She did look nice; the mirror told her so. She hastened out with Eileen to the taxi which, ordered for seven, had been waiting half an hour.

18

When Sally telephoned, Bertram became almost blind with frustrated anger. She said merely that an old friend had suddenly arrived in the neighbourhood and must see her that evening. All Bertram could think of was that he had been cheated.

'Why don't we ask Mrs. Betts to come and make up the numbers?' Shirley suggested.

'That's a good idea.' Bertram decided at once. 'I'll telephone.'

'Perhaps Mrs. Phillips will go and baby-sit with the children after she's finished here,' Shirley said. 'I'll just ask her.'

She went off to do it, and by the time Bertram dialled Eileen's number his rage had passed boiling point and turned to ice. At all costs Marjorie must come; that provocative little bitch Sally should see where her folly led.

The dinner guests began to arrive soon after he had made the telephone call. Hugh Manners was one of the first. He was embarrassed because of Sally's conduct; for once, he had rebuked her and told her that withdrawing so late from the party was too casual. He thought her excuse was inadequate; she had not even had the wit to feign a headache. Shirley was pleased to see him, and brushed aside his excuses for Sally; to her it seemed only natural that the girl should prefer to spend the evening with a contemporary, rather than dutifully among people she met every day.

Hugh's arrival was soon followed by Joan Seabright and her friend Geoffrey Hudson; then came Mr. Thomas, who looked as if he was choking in his stiff white collar. Despite selling men's wear ever since Bliss's had opened the department, he had never learned to fit himself. He was followed by Bertram's meek co-directors and their wives; the men had lost their forcefulness when compelled to sell out, as if they had handed over their manhood with their businesses. Now, secure, they were faceless entities who rarely spoke at meetings and who were perfect foils for Bertram's despotism. Their wives, corseted gushing women with pebble stares and pendant busts, were just as colourless; Shirley wished she could learn to like them; her guilt at feeling such distaste for all of them made her welcome over-effusive.

Soon, Paul arrived with Wendy. They made a striking pair, for he was tall and well built, and his unremarkable face was pleasant enough; and Wendy, with her dark hair dressed high on her head and wearing a dull gold dress, was an arresting sight. Tonight, she was beautiful.

Hugh Manners, who knew Wendy well, soon told her so, and she glowed with pleasure. Her efforts had been successful, it was just unfortunate that the motives that prompted them were not more worthy.

'Where's Sally?' she asked Mr. Manners.

'She isn't coming,' Hugh replied, and explained. Wendy was at once sure that the mysterious friend was Derek. But she embarked loyally upon tactics of diversion, asking about John in Vancouver and talking about a cousin of her own in Winnipeg. Paul hovered on the fringe of this conversation; he was bewildered by Wendy's transformation; he must have been blind before, not to have recognised her potential.

When Eileen and Marjorie appeared at last they made quite an entrance. Any nervousness Marjorie felt soon vanished in the warmth of her welcome. She found herself seated at dinner next to Hugh Manners, who was no stranger; his kind understanding when they met in his office made her feel now that they were friends.

Shirley, at the foot of the table, had Hugh on her right and one of Bertram's co-directors on her left. She was delighted not to be sandwiched between two of these dreary sycophantic men, as was usual. Bertram, of course, had a wife of each on either side; they gazed at him with spaniel eyes which bolstered up his pride and made him as contented, under the circumstances, as was possible. He had not forgiven Sally.

After the meal, the ladies prinked upstairs and put on their coats ready for the journey to The Star. Shirley persuaded Marjorie, before she collected her shabby tweed, to telephone Amanda and make sure the children were all right. They were cheerfully watching television and waiting for Mrs. Phillips to arrive.

At The Star the rank and file of Bliss's were already making merry. The Rocketeers, five youths with purple satin shirts and shaggy heads, were frenetically plucking their electric guitars, trying to 'send' the company, and themselves affecting near-dementia as they writhed and gyrated. Bliss's youngsters jerked, vibrating, on the floor. Hermione Tipps, with her fair hair bleached to ashen white matching her pallid lips, squirmed about opposite young Joe, whose round red face glistened with sweat as he tried to copy her movements. Various older persons sat about on chairs or stood before the bar. When the chairman and his group arrived the musicians played a barely recognisable version of *For He's a Jolly Good Fellow,* which everyone sang with varying degrees of sincerity. When this was ended, Bertram made his usual speech, his annual invitation to every worker to have a splendid time, and 'Thank you for another year of loyal friendship'. To loud applause he took the floor with Shirley, while the guitars did their best to give out *The Blue Danube.*

'He gets away with it all the time,' said Wendy, watching this performance, forgetting that it was Paul who stood beside her, not Sally, the usual participant in strictures about their employer. But Hugh overheard, and cast a sharp glance at the couple moving round the floor. Shirley's crimson skirt swirled by; her head was held high as she stared past Bertram's ear; on spun Bertram, round and round, looking unbearably smug or delightfully genial, according to the viewer's sentiments, and Shirley looked embarrassed.

'Come along, Wendy,' Hugh said, peremptorily, and swept her out to join them on the floor, leaving Paul amazed. Enchanted, Wendy was led around. Hugh was a good dancer in what she thought of as rather a square, old-fashioned way; after several circlings of the floor which drew most of the watching eyes away from Mr. and Mrs. Bliss, Wendy said, 'I wish everyone danced like you do, Mr. Manners. You're wonderful.'

He laughed. 'Bless you, Wendy, what a nice compliment,' he said. 'You've taken years off me. I'm proud to be dancing with the prettiest girl in the room.'

She blushed with pleasure. There was no doubt about it, older men certainly had something.

'In modern dances it makes no difference who your partner is,' she said.

Mr. Manners swirled her round and round.

'It never looks much fun when you see it on television, all that solo dancing miles apart,' he commented.

'It isn't very swoony,' Wendy agreed.

By now other couples had joined them on the floor. Bertram and Shirley were soon lost in a sea of dancers.

'There, my dear, that's enough. Our duty's done,' said Bertram, disengaging her. 'That's got them started.' He shepherded her to the row of chairs at the side of the room, blithely ignoring the fact that his own arrival had damped down the earlier enthusiasm of the revellers. An inhibited staidness now prevailed.

The evening went steadily, relentlessly on, taking its annual course. Shirley was sought by each co-director in his turn, and steered round the room in regal fashion, held in a respectful grip. Knotted in the centre of the floor, a cluster of young people kept up their solo movements, facing each other some of the time, but self-absorbed and often back-to-back.

'Extraordinary, isn't it?' Hugh said, when he danced with Shirley.

'It looks rather mad, I think,' Shirley said. 'And a bit indecent.' She looked hastily away from a particularly energetic exponent of circling hips.

Hugh said: 'Wendy seems to find merit in our more old-fashioned methods.' To his surprise, he found that Shirley danced extremely well; he had not guessed this from watching her with Bertram.

'It seems a bit pointless, all on your own,' she said.

'Not very sociable,' he agreed, and twirled her round in complex manœuvre which she perfectly followed. They both chuckled with pleasure at their skill.

After this first interlude, Hugh danced with her whenever she was free. He was not the least bit interested in any other woman present, and felt no obligation towards them after he had danced with each lady who had been at dinner. He watched Shirley dance with Mr. Thomas, who gritted his teeth and marched her round, oblivious of the music's beat. When she escaped, gasping, from his clutches, Hugh rescued her.

They had danced together four times when Bertram approached them.

'You mustn't get over-tired, dear,' he said to Shirley. 'It's time you went home.'

'I'm not at all tired, Bertie,' Shirley said at once, flushing.

'You know you find these occasions wearing, dear,' Bertram insisted. 'Your duty's done now. Perhaps Mr. Manners would be good enough to run you home. I'm sure he won't wish to be late either. When one is no longer young, one must think of the morrow. I, alas, must remain until the bitter end. Honour demands.'

Hugh could think of several other things honour demanded. Before he could give way to his immediate desire to punch Bertram's nose, he said quickly, 'I'll be happy to take Mrs. Bliss home whenever she is ready to leave.'

'I'm not at all tired, Bertie, really,' Shirley protested.

'Let me have the pleasure of another dance, then,' said Hugh, seizing her, and he swept her off under Bertram's astonished gaze.

'Oh dear,' said Shirley.

'Are you angry with me? Was that very dreadful?'

'No. But I'm vexed with Bertie,' Shirley said, and was amazed at herself for this betrayal.

Hugh gave her a little hug.

'Never mind. Forget it,' he said.

Until tonight, he had forgotten what pleasure could be

found merely in dancing with a woman whose steps matched his. He gave himself up to enjoyment of the moment.

'I have had a nice evening,' Shirley said naively when the dance was done. 'Usually I do get rather bored. Bertie knows that.' Belatedly, she dredged up this minuscule defence.

'So have I,' said Hugh. 'Let's ask the band, or whatever those youths call themselves, to play another waltz; then I'll take you home. That should satisfy everyone.'

'All right,' Shirley agreed. She did not really mind what happened, for it was all the same in the end. Bertram despised her; Hugh saw it, and was being kind.

The group of musicians obeyed the quaint request; Shirley and Hugh danced again, and Bertram went past with Hermione Tipps in his arms, the girl struggling to follow his steps, flushed and awkward.

Finally it ended.

Shirley said, 'If you really don't mind, I'd better go. Bertie likes to be obeyed. But I could get a taxi.'

'What nonsense, of course you won't,' said Hugh. 'I've no desire to stay here without you, Shirley. Get your coat, and by the time you're ready I'll have the car at the door.' He wanted to challenge Bertram by dancing on with this generous, unappreciated woman for what was left of the night, but that would be a stupid satisfaction.

The town was quiet as they drove back, across the bridge and up Castle Hill. Just a few late cars and a cruising taxi went past. The wet weather had broken, and a sharp frost had struck for the last few nights. They drove in silence, comfortably.

'Will you come in?' Shirley asked, when they reached Cedar Grange. He might be bored by now and want to go home.

'Thank you,' he said promptly, and followed her into the house.

A tray with bottles and glasses stood on a table in the living-room; the electric fire gave out a soft glow that took up the warm colour of the curtains.

'Wouldn't you like a drink?' asked Shirley.

'Let me do them,' offered Hugh. 'What will you have?'

'Brandy, please,' said Shirley. She took off her coat and laid it across a chair; then she sat down in her usual place on the sofa. Hugh poured out their drinks and put them on the low coffee-table, then sat beside her.

'This has been a very pleasant evening,' he declared.

'Yes,' said Shirley.

They were silent for a while, but each was content; it was companionable. Then both began to speak at once, and laughed. He waited for her to repeat what she had said.

'I was just asking about your son,' she said. 'When are you going to Vancouver?'

He told her about the vagueness of his plans.

'But I do want Sally to go,' he said. 'I'm afraid she won't, without me. She keeps making silly excuses.'

'You must both go,' said Shirley. 'And send me a post-card of that lovely bridge. What's it called?'

'The Lion's Gate Bridge? Right. That's a promise. And one of the totem poles too. You know they are a great attraction in the city. British Columbia is famous for them.'

'Is it? I didn't know. I've heard it's very lovely,' said Shirley.

'I'll find out all about the totems and how to read the stories they tell, and describe them to you when I get back,' said Hugh. 'In fact, I'll take lots of photographs.'

'Oh do,' said Shirley.

Hugh sipped his drink and glanced at her. The flush that had come to her face in the hot ballroom had faded during their drive, and she was now as pale as she ever looked. In the diffused lighting her face was softened; she looked younger, and vulnerable.

Hugh finished his drink.

'Let me get you another,' he said, holding out his hand for her glass.

'Oh, no,' she began, but he took it and went over to the tray. Shirley heard the clink of glass against glass, then a crash and a muttered oath.

'Blast it ! I've broken a glass. I'm terribly sorry, Shirley,' said Hugh.

'Goodness, it doesn't matter,' said Shirley, getting up. She crossed the room to Hugh, who stood holding his hand.

'You've cut yourself.'

'It's nothing.' Hugh lifted the handkerchief he had pressed against his finger, and revealed a spurt of blood.

'Let me see,' she commanded, and bent to inspect the damage. 'You must put something on it.'

'It's perfectly all right,' Hugh repeated. 'It'll stop bleeding in a minute. What a mess I've made.'

'Never mind about the glass,' said Shirley. 'The store is full of them. Bertie could bring a hundred back tomorrow and never notice. It's your hand that matters.' She was holding it by now. 'You'd better come upstairs,' she said. 'I'll find some Elastoplast.'

He followed her meekly through the hall, up the open-treaded staircase, along the landing, through her apricot bedroom and into the bathroom beyond, then stood, obedient, while she bathed the cut. It was not deep, but was one of those superficial ones that bleed a lot until the sides are forced together.

'It can't be dirty,' he objected, when she insisted on washing it out with Dettol. 'There was only brandy in the glass. That's a prize disinfectant.'

'It's better to be sure,' said Shirley. Bowed over his hand, ministering to him, she wound the plaster firmly in position, holding it in place to make sure it had adhered.

'There, that should stay on,' she pronounced at last.

He said, 'You're a remarkable woman.'

'Oh heavens, why?' Shirley asked. She began to move out of the bathroom, and he followed, his wounded finger extended.

'You're far too humble,' said Hugh. 'You're an excellent driver, you dance like an angel, you run a lovely home and you turn to in the store when things are difficult, yet you've no conceit. And you make not the slightest fuss about a broken glass and a possibly damaged carpet.'

Shirley looked at him uncertainly, a little bewildered by this outburst.

'Your finger was what mattered,' she said.

'I like your dress,' he said, inconsequentially as it seemed to her.

'Your daughter chose the colour.'

'Well, good for her.' Hugh advanced a pace, and Shirley stood quite still. She could not believe what her senses told her was about to happen.

'You're a fine and lovely woman,' Hugh declared.

It would be impolite to move away. Besides, she did not want to. She stood fast, and he took her hands.

'And I think you're rather lonely, like me,' he added. Then, very gently, he kissed her.

Everything telescoped for Shirley. She felt no pang of conscience, only mild surprise at how easy and how natural it seemed as she moved into Hugh's arms.

Bertie would not be back for hours.

19

Soon after ten o'clock, Paul Jessamy suggested to Wendy that they should leave the heat and congestion of the Star ballroom and go into the hotel itself where, in the Constellation Bar, they might enjoy a quiet drink in a rarer atmosphere. So it was that they spent some time drinking Bloody Marys, seated in deep leather chairs in a cocktail lounge which was illumined by heavenly bodies suspended from a metal ceiling, and where the carpet was, like the night sky, midnight blue. While they sipped their drinks, Paul told Wendy all about his home and family, which she knew already, but she listened patiently. She had resolved to dazzle him tonight, and because it was clear that she was easily succeeding, her confidence grew with every minute so that she dazzled still more.

Paul made no attempt to resist; soon the opposite became his one aim, and when Wendy had listened for half an hour to the story of his life with apparent rapt attention, he proposed that as the night was fine, they should go for a drive.

The sky was clear, and the headlights of Paul's car sent silver probes into the darkness. Wendy, wrapped like a chrysalis in her fun-fur coat, wondered if she would have the expertise to carry out her plan, while Paul pondered the best tactics for his.

They crossed the bridge, and climbed up Castle Hill beyond the houses and into the higher open country. They did not talk. Outside the car, the bare-branched trees and hedgerows glistened with frost; the pale moon shone, and the road sparkled with rime. After a while Paul slowed down and took the car off the road into a lay-by. It was a well-chosen spot, with an impressive view of the lighted town, the glinting river, and, beyond, the coast. Admiring this made a topic of conversation while Paul experimentally put his left arm round Wendy and turned her towards him.

Play it cool, she thought, wondering if she would be able to control what followed. She allowed herself to be slowly moved to face him. Part of her wanted to laugh, but she was excited too. Pretty speeches did not come easily to Paul, and he was not imaginative; in silence he slid his left hand up to the back of her head so that she could not easily retreat, and kissed her. He was gentle, because apprehensive in case she objected, but she responded with what seemed to Paul amazing ardour. Encouraged, he grew bolder.

After a while he let her go.

'Let's go back to my place,' he suggested. 'You'll get cold here.'

Wendy mumbled agreement. It had not been difficult to play her part so far. She was slightly shocked at her own conduct, but intoxicated by her sense of power. She let her hand rest on Paul's knee as they drove back down the hill and through the town to The Grove. She would have to hope for inspiration as to how to manipulate the next round.

Paul parked outside the house where he lived and helped her out of the car. It was a large old detached house, built before the stucco semi-detached row in the same road occupied by the Betts family. Paul led Wendy in, and up the stairs. He had a large room on the top floor. On the way, they passed the bathroom; she could see it as they went by for the door was ajar; when they reached Paul's landing he showed her the small kitchen at the end of the passage which he shared with the two other tenants on this floor. They reached the door of his room and he released her hand, which he had been holding all this time, to unlock it.

Paul did not turn on the main light when they entered

his room, but crossed to a table near the fire where he put down his keys and switched on a red-shaded lamp which cast a rosy glow over a limited area. Then he lit the gas fire. Wendy looked curiously round. The walls were papered with a modern design; a cubist chair such as they sold in the store faced the hearth; and the usual divan, but with a black linen fitted cover and bright scarlet cushions, was against one wall. There were a few pictures on the wall, but she could not distinguish them clearly in the subdued light; they seemed to be abstracts. Her quick glance did not note a kettle, nor a ring of any sort. All cooking arrangements must be carried out in the kitchen.

She shivered elaborately.

'It will soon warm up,' said Paul, rising from his attentions to the fire. He advanced towards her, wearing a smug and fatuous expression. The conceit of it! All guilt about her intentions vanished. 'Let me warm you,' Paul was muttering, reaching inside her coat. She swayed towards him and closed her eyes. For a few minutes she pretended he was Albert Finney. It worked quite well, and she heard his breathing quicken as he felt for the zip at the back of her dress.

It was time to shiver again. She did so, vigorously.

'I'm sorry, Paul, I'm still cold. Do you think we could have some coffee, or something hot?' she asked.

'Of course, darling. I'm sorry, I should have thought of it,' he said. 'You stay by the fire and I'll make it. I'll be very quick.' He kissed her again, and reluctantly released her.

When he had gone, Wendy buttoned up her coat again, picked up the car keys from the table where Paul had put them, and followed him from the room. She could hear him clattering about in the kitchen at the end of the passage, and put her head round the door.

'I'm just popping down to the bathroom,' she told him.

'Right,' he said, standing with a cup in one hand and what she thought of as his silly grin on his face. Already the kettle was humming on the stove.

Wendy went down the stairs, opened the bathroom door wide and closed it firmly, then continued on silently till she reached the hall. She let herself soundlessly out of the house and tiptoed along the path into the road. Then she picked up her skirt and ran, in her high-heeled shoes, to the corner where The Grove joined the main road. Paul would not miss her for some minutes, at least. He probably had a spare key for his car, but finding it would take time; she could count on a ten-minute start. She would have taken his car, but alas, she could not drive.

The buses had ceased to run now; her plan, such as it was, had been to telephone for a taxi from the nearest call-box, but luck was with her; an empty one came cruising along as she hurried down the road, and by the time that Paul realised she had vanished she was in her own room. She could trust her intransigent landlady to fend off an importunate Paul if he were to follow.

Paul waited for her to return to his room for nearly a quarter of an hour, with the coffee steadily cooling all the while. At last he went downstairs and called her name softly, outside the bathroom. He called again, several times, before he tried the door, opened it, and saw that she had gone.

At first he believed that he had mislaid his keys; in his haste to be alone with Wendy he must have dropped them somewhere. Eventually he found the spare, and set off in pursuit.

At Wendy's house he was told by an irate elderly woman, her grey wispy hair twisted in curlers, who answered his ring, that Miss Brown had returned alone some time ago and was by now asleep, as all right-minded people should be at this hour, and as she had been herself until disturbed. Under no circumstances whatever might he be permitted to enter the house.

Paul returned slowly to The Grove in a state of bewildered anger. Never in his life before had he felt such total humiliation, nor been so bitter with rage.

20

Meanwhile, the revellers at The Star continued to dance out the hours, and others dreamed of conquest. One who did not, Mr. Thomas, could by eleven o'clock endure no more; he asked Miss Westcott if she was ready to leave; his duty would not be fully discharged until she had been safely delivered home.

Eileen looked about for Marjorie and saw her with Bertram, sipping a drink that looked like ginger ale but might be much more potent. When Eileen explained that she was going, Marjorie at once said that she would come too.

'No, no, Mrs. Betts. Don't spoil your drink by hurrying,' Bertram admonished. 'I'll take you home presently.'

'Yes, you stay,' urged Eileen. Marjorie was clearly enjoying herself and it would be a pity to drag her away. 'I'll see that the children are all right and send Mrs. Phillips home.'

She left with Mr. Thomas, sedately, in a taxi, and the dance went on; people began to drift away, but many still remained. Bertram's co-directors and their wives tripped on, circling round and round; the Rocketeers played indefatigably and the lights were dimmed.

At length the last waltz was traditionally played and

the couples on the floor clasped one another in varying degrees of cohesion. Hermione and Joe, eyes shut, blundered about in trance-like joy; Hermione had forgotten all about Paul. Finally *Auld Lang Syne* was twangily played by the group and sung in sentimental, slurring voices by those who were left. There was a hectic, sometimes embarrassing, exchange of kisses, and in the resulting tumult Bertram led Marjorie away.

'I have had a lovely time,' she told him as she sank back in the now familiar Rover.

'I hope tonight marks the start of a happier chapter of your life,' Bertram said.

They drove out of The Star yard, through a cluster of departing employees who waved, and even gave a few tipsy cheers as the chairman's car cleft its passage smoothly through their midst.

'Would you care to come in, Mr. Bliss?' Marjorie asked timidly, when they reached the house, glad at last to be in a position to be able to suggest it. 'Perhaps you would like some tea?'

'That would be quite delightful,' said Bertram at once.

Marjorie felt proud, leading him in. He had often come before, of course, but as Eileen's guest; now, here was her chance to repay some of his kindness by a little hospitality. She took him into the sitting-room. The fire, kept in throughout the evening by Mrs. Phillips while she gazed at television, had burnt low but still glowed red. Marjorie crouched before it and put on bits of coal, then took the bellows to revive it. Watching her curving back and neat movements, Bertram was sharply reminded of Sally. Thus had she knelt before the fire at Warren End, the day he had driven her home from the station.

'Let me do that while you make the tea,' said Bertram, crossing the room. He took the bellows from her and squatted down before the grate. It was the first time for years that he had undertaken so domestic a task.

Marjorie went to the kitchen and hummed softly under her breath as she laid a tray with Eileen's best china. She moved quietly, though Michael, in the dining-room, was a sound sleeper. When she got back to the sitting-room Bertram had put a small table before the sofa ready to receive the tray, which he now took from her and set down, and the fire was blazing. Marjorie seated herself behind the tray and poured out; Bertram sat at her side.

While they drank their tea Bertram asked about the children and their progress, and she replied with eager accounts of all their hopes and plans.

'It is a grief to me to have no children,' Bertram said sadly, putting down his empty cup and moving the table further from the sofa so that there was freedom to manœuvre. 'I envy you yours.'

'Yes,' said Marjorie. She looked at him with sympathy. 'How sad for you.'

'Well, it was not to be. My wife, you know . . .' His voice trailed off, leaving her imagination to finish the sentence.

Marjorie, embarrassed, drank the rest of her tea with a gulp and then leaned forward to put the cup down on the tray, now almost out of reach. How very distressing for him, the kindest among men, to have no one to succeed him in the business, no stake in posterity. They sat in silence for a while, in respectful tribute to what might have been.

At length Bertram spoke.

'I want you to come into the office next month and work with Mrs. Seabright,' he told her. 'She will be joining the board shortly, and will have less time for routine work. We are hoping to expand still further. She tells me you have secretarial experience. You will be Mrs. Seabright's and my personal secretary and assistant, and your salary will commence at nine hundred pounds a year.'

To Marjorie, it sounded as if she had been given the freedom of the Bank of England.

'But I've forgotten all my shorthand!' she exclaimed.

'You'll soon get it back,' he assured her. 'In any case, you won't require it much. I often use a dictaphone. Mrs. Seabright will help you recover your skills, rest assured.'

'Oh, Mr. Bliss!' She gazed at him. 'You have been good to me.' Her eyes brimmed with tears. 'Where would we be now, but for you?'

'Come now, we can't have tears, that well never do.' Bertram took a spotless handkerchief from his pocket, moved close to her, and gently dabbed at her face. Laughing sheepishly, she took the handkerchief herself and dried her eyes. Bertram's arm lay at her back, across the sofa.

'You must think me very silly. I'm sorry. Really, I don't know what to say,' she said. 'I can never thank you enough.'

He rested his hand lightly on her shoulder. She did not seem to notice.

'I think you're charming, and deserve a little aid,' he declared, and drew still nearer. 'Life has been cruel to you long enough.'

Marjorie was scarcely aware of his physical presence; all that she could think of was his kindness; he was her saviour. She had forgotten what could follow merely from sitting on a sofa with a man. When he held her more tightly and moved closer still, she thought he was simply being fatherly.

'Very charming,' he repeated, and now something in his voice did startle her. She saw his eyes, pale and protuberant, very near, and suddenly his mouth, warm and wet, was laid upon her icy, frightened lips.

She sprang away at once, out of his grip and out of range, appalled.

'No, no!' she cried, drawing her hand across her mouth.

She tried, belatedly, to remember that this assaulter was her boss, to whom was due her gratitude if nothing else.

Bertram's concern for his own dignity came immediately to the rescue.

'There's no need to be alarmed,' he said austerely. 'A salutation between friends is not an insult.'

'No, no, I didn't mean . . .' Marjorie was shaking. How could she explain that the degradation she had undergone in her married life had made her unable to contemplate physical contact with a demanding male? Doubtless she had misunderstood his action; doubtless it was done in friendship, as he said, and not in urgency; but on her the effect was just the same.

'It was so kind of you to bring me home, Mr. Bliss. I'm sorry,' she said, and looked at him with the expression of a cringing, terrified dog.

Bertram got up, said a cold good night, and left, immediately re-writing in his mind the recent minutes till he was sure his kiss had merely been a chaste salute.

Marjorie, when he had gone, shivered and shook. What would happen now? Would he take back his offer of a better job? Should she accept it if it was confirmed? Did he expect her gratitude to be expressed in intimacy? Had she really misunderstood?

21

Afterwards, Shirley could hardly believe that it had happened. So gentle an encounter must have been imagined. But she remembered its inevitability, and her awareness that retreat would not have been an act of merit. She had met sudden, tender humour with responding joy. In the days that followed she smiled often in recollection, and would glance at Bertram as he cut up his food or studied his stamps, and marvel that he sensed no change. Because he no longer wanted her, he would never think another man might find in her something to admire. She grew daily more critical of Bertram. The sound of his step ceased to be something she listened for; the preparation of choice meals and the care of the house no longer pleased her. When she thought about her life the prospect of the future appalled her.

Slowly, as she viewed Bertram more objectively, a new appreciation of her own identity began to grow, and before Hugh and Sally left for Vancouver she had ceased to think of herself any longer as an adjunct to Bertram; she, too, was an individual.

Some time before they left, the Manners gave a small party to which Shirley and Bertram were invited. Shirley felt a calm pleasure when she saw Hugh again. There was no need for any shame.

'When do you leave?' she asked, and listened to their plans. They were flying out, pausing for one night on the way in Toronto, where Hugh had a friend, but they planned to return across Canada by train, so as to see as much of the country as they could through the observation dome. So early in the year, though, much of the land would still be under snow.

'You'll go again,' said Shirley. 'Sally, you should stay over there.'

'Oh, no. I must keep an eye on my old dad,' said Sally with a laugh. She left them, and crossed the room to talk to someone else.

'I must make her leave me soon,' said Hugh.

'Yes,' said Shirley. 'It'll be harder, the longer you leave it.'

'I suppose so. I've been marking time long enough as it is,' said Hugh.

Shirley knew, when they parted, that their miraculous brief moment of communion would not occur again. Now they were friends, and that was all there would ever be.

She began to assert herself in mild ways. She visited the store whenever she felt like doing so, touring round the departments making herself familiar with the stock and known to each employee. When Bertram protested she reminded him that she owned over half the shares and had every right, if not a duty, to know what was going on. She resigned from the Townswomen's Guild and accepted the post of secretary to the Floral Art Society, together with the apologies of Lady Murcott for making the initial arrangements for the spring fashion show without her. She went to London and stayed for three days, during which time she bought clothes, had her hair cut short, went to the cinema and the National Gallery and the theatre, and booked herself a single first-class cabin on a cruise to Greece the following May.

Bertram never quarrelled openly. When he found he could not stop this little rebellion he nodded sagely, decided that her restlessness was a manifestation of her age, and ignored it.

One February day, when it was freezing hard outside and the skies were grey, Shirley bent to pick up a pencil she had dropped. As she stooped, she felt suddenly giddy. She took some deep breaths and sat down, and was soon all right again. A few mornings later she woke feeling sick. She thought it must be due to something she had eaten the night before; the feeling passed off quickly and she forgot about it. But the next morning, and the next, and the morning after, she felt sick again, and heaved in the bathroom, mopping her eyes and clutching her stomach, while Bertram, unaware, lay drinking his tea in their apricot bed.

On the fifth morning she was ready, and muffled her

symptoms, but she need not have worried, for Bertram noticed nothing. When he left for work she went back to the bedroom and looked at herself in the mirror. She was rather pale, and there were circles under her eyes, but she looked very well.

It could not be true.

Anyway, she was too old.

It was just not possible.

The next day, after she had been sick again, she went to the public library and consulted the medical directory. Then she telephoned London for an appointment with a gynaecologist she had thus discovered.

A few days later she went to London once again.

After a prolonged examination the doctor sat behind his desk, beaming at her.

'Well, Mrs. Bliss, you are pregnant,' he told her. 'There's no doubt of that.'

Shirley sat submissively, having her blood pressure taken and being told that in spite of her age there was no reason for anxiety. She hardly heard what was said. She agreed to come back in a fortnight's time for a further check and to make plans for the delivery. Then she left, in a daze, and walked off up the road in the general direction of Regent's Park. There she sat on a bench, wrapped in her mink, gazing at the dull winter grass and the bare-branched trees, trying to absorb the truth.

In October the baby would be born. Spring would come, then summer, then, with the falling leaves, her baby.

Shirley had been married for twenty-three years. For almost all that time she had lived with the conviction that it was her failure to conceive that had prevented her and Bertram from raising a family. Now, suddenly, the belief of half a lifetime had been swept away. Slowly, while she sat there, oblivious of the cold wind and the threat of snow, numbness began to depart and new sensations took its place, keener than any she had felt for years: awe, and exaltation. Then, as well, came anger. Bertram had been too proud to admit that the fault could be his, and too obstinate to find out; he had been content for her, all this time, to bear the blame.

What could he say now?

At last, reluctantly, she realised that she must contrive things so that Bertram would believe the child to be his. The thought filled her with a strange repugnance. She got up from the bench and walked along a path, thinking. It must, somehow, be done; it was the only way.

She travelled home in the train, planning how the small spare room could be re-furnished and painted white, with a frieze of ducks upon the wall.

22

'His wife had been trying to find him for hours,' Sally said. She sat perched on her stool, clasping her knees with her hands. 'It was dreadful.'

'What happened?' Wendy stood at her bench, surrounded by yellow crêpe paper and the cardboard outlines of lambs. Both girls were trying, with scant enthusiasm, to prepare window decorations to greet the spring, which on this dull grey day seemed impossibly distant. 'Was he badly hurt?'

'He's broken a leg, and at first they were afraid he'd fractured his skull, but luckily it was only concussion,' said Sally. 'He'll be in hospital for quite a while.'

'Poor little kid. But it wasn't your fault,' said Wendy.

'I feel as if it was,' Sally said.

On the night of the dance, Derek had telephoned. He had been to a wedding not far from Sedgemouth; at the last minute Angela had elected not to come, because one of the boys was not very well. Derek had escaped the post-wedding revels for which Angela supposed him to be staying on, with the plea of hurrying back to London. He had taken Sally to a small village on the coast where they had spent the night in an old, cosy pub, insulated from the winter and the intrusions of their other lives.

When Derek got back to London on Sunday afternoon he had found Angela nearly hysterical. That morning the *au pair* girl had gone to church, and while Angela tended the invalid, Garry had opened the garden gate, ridden his tricycle into the road and been hit by a passing car which had no chance to avoid him. Angela had telephoned around to try and trace Derek, but was told he had left to return home the evening before. At first she thought he, too, had met with an accident. Her relief at his appearance was shot through with anger.

'It would have happened even if Derek had been at home,' said Wendy.

'No. He'd have seen the gate was properly shut. Anyway, he'd have been there to help, if it had happened,' said Sally. 'Suppose Garry had been killed?' She still felt, vicariously, the horror Angela must have experienced that morning. 'And he had meant to go straight back. That was why he didn't telephone me before. But then he decided it was too good a chance to miss.'

Wendy said, briskly, 'Well, Garry wasn't killed, and it's no good going on torturing yourself about it because you've got a guilty conscience. It could have happened any time, when Derek was at work.'

Sally thought of the story Derek had told his wife: the tale of going on from the wedding with an old friend and drinking too much at a pub on the way to London, then staying the night. It was a poor, thin fable; it had deceived

Angela briefly, but she might doubt it later on when she had got over her shock and had time to reflect. Neither it, nor the truth, was a pretty story.

Sally said, 'Well, I suppose brooding helps no one. What about you? Doesn't your conscience prick just a bit? Poor Paul, I should think you've dealt his pride a mortal blow.'

Wendy giggled.

'It'll recover, you'll see,' she said. 'He deserved it.'

'You're too hard on him,' said Sally, who thought Wendy had gone too far. She had never seen Paul as any sort of Casanova; his approach to her had always been diffident.

'Anyway, Hermione and Joe are engaged, it seems, so I need not have bothered on her account,' said Wendy.

'A pretty swift rebound. What an exciting time you all had,' said Sally. 'Father seems to have enjoyed it. He's full of new plans and ploys since that night. Thank goodness he's decided to go to John's wedding.' She picked up a sheet of cardboard. 'I'm going to draw some gorgeous golden Wordsworthian daffodils. You'd better brace up, Wendy. All will depend on you while I'm in Canada. I hope you enjoy your conclaves with Babs.'

'I can't think why you don't look for a job in Canada, while you have the chance,' said Wendy. 'Your brother's in-laws would help, wouldn't they? It wouldn't be like going into the unknown. You'd have a marvellous time and meet lots of husky men in plaid shirts.' And soon forget Derek, she thought.

'Canadians aren't all trappers or lumbermen, you know,' Sally said, austerely. She loaded her paintbrush with yellow and began to block in her daffodil.

Meanwhile, down in the basement, Paul Jessamy was a subdued young man these days. His assistant Joe, happy and besotted with Hermione, tended to whistle at work and had to be subdued. Marjorie Betts, so valuable in

Lighting, had been wafted aloft to the offices and a new saleslady, stout and slow-moving, was in her place. The year stretched bleakly ahead of him, with no exciting landmarks to anticipate; there would be the spring furnishing campaign, the summer sales, autumn, and another year would end with an exaggerated Christmas season once again. Nothing would be changed. He sighed as he worked; for the first time in his career the increased turnover in his department failed to thrill. On the social front, where once he had loitered to catch a glimpse of Sally, now he spent his time dodging Wendy, for he did not wish to be reminded of the way that she had mocked him. If they had to meet, he ignored her unless obliged to speak, and if this happened he used the minimum words and addressed the air above her head. Wendy watched these manœuvres with malicious delight and took pleasure in ambushing Paul, to disconcert him; she had no pity.

At this time, Marjorie Betts was one of the most contented employees in the store. She worked, now, alongside Joan Seabright, growing daily more skilled with the electric typewriter and more rapid with her shorthand. She had assumed a new personality, quiet and self-effacing as before, but no longer cowed. An altered relationship had developed between her and Bertram; it was formal, courteous, remote. Marjorie strove for efficiency, and Bertram tended his dignity. He no longer drove her or Eileen home. After the dance, Marjorie had pulled down a blind in her mind, refusing to admit the memory of Bertram's flushed, importunate face, and he, with his usual ease, had entirely obliterated all recollection of his rebuff.

As the calm days passed, Marjorie put on weight, the children gained in health and spirits, and their work at school improved. Peter Betts, dismayed at the prospect of a squalid suit against him, had provided evidence for a neat divorce; the bitterness of years could be left unstirred.

He had moved to another job in Manchester. The children did not seem to miss their father; he had never been a dependable factor in their lives. They grew fond of Eileen, called her 'Auntie', and trusted her. They felt secure.

Joan Seabright appreciated the lightening of her load brought by Marjorie's assistance. She even found that she did not mind Marjorie's presence in her office, something she had expected to resent; Marjorie was so quiet that she was barely noticeable. Now, with more time, Joan had embarked on an intensive advertising campaign; new, bright features in the local papers and even in the cinemas publicised the wares of Bliss.

One day, going to the Stork Bar to select some items to push in the weekend press, Joan found Shirley there, dreaming over a yellow-trimmed cot and holding a woolly rabbit in her hand. The encounter in this department was rather surprising to Joan, but she knew that Shirley had spent a lot of time in the store lately; she had made some shrewd suggestions about eliminating waste which Bertram had been forced to accept. Doubtless her interest extended to every area.

'It's pretty, isn't it?' Joan said, admiring the cot. 'Shall I give it a splash in *The Echo*?'

'Why not? But I expect it would sell in any case,' said Shirley.

'I don't know. Most young couples seem to plump for something more practical, like a carry-cot,' said Joan. 'This is the type of thing grandmothers buy.'

'I suppose you're right.' Shirley put the rabbit into the cot. 'Well, I mustn't waste any more time,' she said vaguely, and went away, leaving Joan to the plastic animals and the stretchy playsuits so popular today.

23

Shirley's euphoric state endured for nearly a week. In that time the days passed filled with dreams, but at night the need to seduce Bertram filled her with dread. For a long time now they had exchanged no more than a perfunctory kiss; she supposed she had no more charm for him; it did not occur to her to question his ability. He lay with his back towards her every night, remote and unapproachable. Once she put out a tentative hand and touched him. He merely grunted.

'What's the matter? Can't you sleep?' he asked.

Shirley withdrew again to her own half of their enormous bed. She had never in all the years flung herself upon him in abandonment, merely seeking to follow, willingly enough, where he led; she could not alter now.

Another week wouldn't make much difference. At her age a miscalculation could be easily explained. If she assumed reluctance Bertram might, contrariwise, develop ardour. She pushed the thought of what must be done to the back of her mind.

But soon reaction set in. Shirley's delight diminished as she began to think in more practical terms about the future. Joan's remark about grandmothers buying frilly cots made her aware that by rights this should be her role; by the time the child was adult she would be approaching seventy. But still, she told herself, elderly parents were common enough these days, and at least shortage of cash was something that need not be feared. The child would lack for nothing. Some sort of trustee arrangement must be made, in case anything happened to her.

This made her think of lawyers, and at last of Hugh. So far she had completely ignored his part in all this;

she had been concerned solely with the baby and herself.

The child might look like him.

Would anyone notice, if this happened?

At last she admitted to herself that, inevitably, Hugh would work it out. Even if Bertram were deceived, Hugh would know. She had not a single qualm about Bertram, but she felt a great sense of responsibility towards Hugh. Now her joy dwindled and disappeared as she saw how he could be affected. He would feel under an obligation to her; he would have an interest in the child, and a right to it, and the child would have a right to know his father. There was Sally, too. It was not as though she and Hugh were ardently in love; she did not deceive herself about that.

She contemplated telling Hugh, and even, on a flimsy excuse, went round to Warren End. But preparations for the trip to Canada were under way; Hugh was checking lists, loading his camera, consulting maps, and unable to think of anything else. Shirley could not shatter him with her news. She thought he had probably forgotten all about their little interlude. It would be wrong to inflate such a fleeting encounter into an affair of passion, which it would seem if a scandal resulted. Hugh could be ruined by such a thing in this provincial town, and Bertram would be a figure of fun. Nothing justified this risk.

She began to plan afresh. She would provoke an open quarrel with Bertram and leave him. She would go to some remote place in Cornwall, have the baby and bring him up in obscurity alone. She could sell her holding in the store; goodness knows, the large groups often enough asked her to do so; later she could set up in business on her own and build up something for her child to inherit. She could dispose of her own shares how she liked; the terms of the agreement drawn up when her father and Bertram formed the company together allowed her absolute freedom; only Bertram could not sell his without her approval. In this way Harry Hawkins, ashamed of his suspicions yet never wholly happy about what had caused the fire that burnt his shop out, had sought to protect his only daughter.

Shirley developed this idea for some days; she even consulted travel books in the local library about the Cornish peninsula, and thought that Truro would be nice.

But she could not disappear without a trace. She would be tracked down. The baby would be discovered.

She could pretend to have adopted him. She might have to do this anyway, for the child's own sake.

She would never get away with it. The way the world wagged, Hugh would know. In the end it came to this: Hugh must never find out.

It took her still a few more days to accept what must be done. She cancelled her second appointment with the London doctor and sat for hours in the little bedroom, mourning in advance.

These things could be arranged, but how? Who would know?

Sally, leading her off-beat life, might, but could not possibly be asked. Anyway, she was now in Canada.

Joan was another woman of experience, but Shirley could not imagine discussing such a thing with her, no matter how clever a tale she told.

Eileen could be consulted, but would she know the answer? It seemed unlikely. But people were unfathomable; Shirley remembered the soldier's photograph. Eileen had friends she did not know about; she might have sources.

She invited her to lunch at *The Copper Kettle,* and over roast lamb and redcurrant jelly told her a story about a mythical friend who lived on Castle Hill and had a daughter who was in trouble; she was in the middle of her college career and had to be rescued.

Eileen looked curiously at Shirley, who seemed so concerned for this girl whom she had never talked about before. She made suggestions about adoption and so forth, but Shirley rejected them at once; there was no choice, she said. At length Eileen admitted that she had a friend who knew someone who had had an abortion. She would make enquiries.

Committed to this doubtful course, Eileen wasted no time. In a few days she told Shirley where the girl could go. During this short interval Shirley's whole mood changed. She refused to entertain emotion. She had made her decision and must carry it out, however difficult and frightening it was. And she would never forgive Bertram.

He did not seem to notice her withdrawal. He was melancholy because Sally was away, and instead of living up to her former promise Wendy seemed vague and uninspired. The truth was that without Sally she lost drive. Together, the girls struck sparks off one another, but Sally was always the first to start the fire.

When Shirley said she was going to London again for a few days Bertram looked surprised but gave her only part of his attention.

'You're always going to London now,' he said. 'Hasn't Sedgemouth enough to offer you?'

'No,' said Shirley firmly. 'Sedgemouth is provincial.' She added that she would be back in plenty of time to make the final arrangements for the fashion show with her Floral Art group. 'I want it to be a success,' she said.

'Of course it will be that,' said Bertram. With his hand behind it, how could it be otherwise?

Shirley looked at him. She did not even hate him; it was too much trouble. She despised him. She deplored all the wasted years that were gone, spent, she realised now, in a state of suspended growth where she was concerned. But things would change. She had made her plans.

24

Sally walked into the vast, panelled hall of the Priory and stared amazed. The huge room was filled with purposeful women padding to and fro with controlled urgency. There were muted sounds to be heard : the snapping of secateurs, the splitting of stems, and the splosh of water poured from one vessel to another. An acute ear might detect the rasp of wire netting being crushed into bundles and wedged into containers. Under the soaring hammer-beamed roof, the ladies of the Floral Art Society were making ready for their first big occasion of the year. The Priory was to display their handiwork as a background for a fashion show. By such means, giving creative plea-sure to themselves and visual joy to others, the ladies raised throughout the year impressive sums for charity.

In every vantage point of the public rooms in the large, rambling old house a vase was placed. Some were already filled with towering blooms : forced lilac, early irises, daffodils and tulips, blossom and young foliage stood on tables, chests, and in alcoves. As they finished their work the ladies began to talk; the murmur of voices grew louder, and there came the occasional sound of a tense laugh. Then followed the clank of brush and dustpan as they removed the traces of their labours from the polished floor.

At first Sally could recognise no one. She looked around at the vivid displays of colour, then at the figures moving about. At last she identified Shirley's rear view. Kneeling on a dustsheet, she was collecting up a pile of twigs, leaves and broken stems. Above her bent head, on a tall Georgian wig stand, was arranged a bowl of daffodils and forsythia, rising into a fan of yellow against the dark panelling of the wall behind.

'That's beautiful, Mrs. Bliss,' Sally said.

Shirley sat back on her heels. With her hair cut short she appeared quite different, younger and more sophisticated. She looked pale, and was thinner than Sally remembered.

'Why, Sally! What are you doing here? I thought you were still in Canada,' said Shirley.

Sally squatted down on hands and knees beside Shirley.

'Let me help you clear this up,' she said. 'The flowers are truly gorgeous.' She gathered up a pile of slimy daffodil stems. 'I came back earlier than originally planned,' she said. 'Father's staying on a bit. He's going to live it up in Toronto.'

Sally helped Shirley wrap her bits and pieces into some sheets of newspaper, and held them while Shirley rolled up the dustsheet and stuffed it into the basket in which she had brought her flowers.

'Was it wonderful? Have you had a lovely time?'

'It was tremendous,' said Sally. 'What a country. It's just so vast, you can't really imagine it without seeing it. At least, I couldn't. Of course, we weren't there at the best time of year, but it was marvellous. Vancouver's lovely. A white city, with the Rockies in the background. We took lots of photographs.'

'I hope you're going to show them to me,' said Shirley. 'I didn't believe you'd come back, Sally. It must be a splendid place for young people.'

'Oh, it is. Lots of opportunity and masses of space. But England has its charms.' Sally looked round the room. 'This, for instance. You wouldn't find anything quite like this over there.'

Most of the tidying-up was done now, and two men in aprons appeared to arrange the chairs on which tomorrow's audience was to sit.

'I've been over to the store,' Sally said. 'Miss Westcott's got 'flu and can't do the commentary, so Mr. Bliss asked me to take her place. It'll be fun. There are some wonderful clothes, and three models all of different ages. Oh, I suppose you know all about it, Mrs. Bliss.'

'Well, I've seen what's going to be shown,' said Shirley.

'I thought I'd have an advance look round,' Sally said. 'I've never done anything like this before. The microphone won't be set up till tomorrow, I suppose.'

'No. In the morning, some time. And we'll all be here again by then, filling up our vases and cutting sandwiches,' said Shirley. 'Come and look at the flowers.'

They walked together through the rooms of the old house where the models would parade the following day. Sally thought that some of the arrangements were too contrived, nature sacrificed to artifice, but they were lovely nevertheless. She decided that she would enjoy her part of the proceedings; it would be almost her swan-song for the store, for she was leaving Bliss's.

Late one night in Vancouver she had gazed from her bedroom window at the lighted city, shining reflected in its surrounding water. Soon it would be dawn in England, where Derek was. Strange to think of him getting up now, going to work, while she prepared for sleep.

Nothing that parted her from him was worth her while.

She would go back to England at once, hand in her notice with no more delay, and find a job in London. This would make meeting Derek easy. She saw no happy outcome; he might tire of her, or of deception, or the claims of his family might prove too great, but until that happened, this was the only choice she had. And in London she would be able to find a job that offered her more scope than Bliss's; she might develop a real career in commercial art, and this would compensate for much that might be lacking in her life.

She saw that her father could spare her now; and she had fresh hope for him. On the plane flying out they had met a pretty, grey-haired widow with merry blue eyes and

179

pink cheeks. She and Hugh had stared at one another, gasped, and realised that they had known each other in their youth. Elspeth Harris was on her way to visit her married daughter in Toronto. Hugh secured her address, both in England and in Canada, and they agreed to meet.

Hugh had airily announced his intention of spending a few days in Toronto on his way home, just to look round, for twenty-four hours on the outward journey was not much. Later, if he was alone at Warren End, he might have an extra incentive to seek out Elspeth. One could not be sure if anything would come of it, but there was just a chance.

Sally told Shirley that she was leaving Bliss's.

'Oh, Sally, we'll miss you,' Shirley said at once. 'But you're right to go, my dear. There's no more for you here. You should be able to get a very interesting job in London.'

'Father can manage now,' said Sally. 'Anyway, I can keep an eye on him at weekends.'

'I'm sure he'll be all right,' said Shirley. 'Where will you live and what will you do?'

'I'm going to look for a tiny flat, if I can find a job that will pay enough,' said Sally. 'Advertising, I thought. Or possibly public relations. I'm not sure. I'll have to look about. It's exciting.'

'Yes,' said Shirley. 'Quite a challenge.' She hesitated, glanced at Sally, then decided to plunge. 'I'm branching out too,' she said. 'I'm opening a boutique. It's a secret still, so please don't tell anyone.'

'Of course I won't! How marvellous, Mrs. Bliss. What a good idea. Where? In Sedgemouth?'

'Yes. I've found a place in Cutler Street,' said Shirley. 'I'm going to stock expensive clothes for people like tomorrow's audience, and difficult sizes, and scarves and so on. Things that are just a little bit more exclusive than the normal scope of the store.'

'Will it be part of Bliss's?' Sally asked.

'No,' said Shirley. 'This is my own pet project. My baby, you might say. I'm going to call it *Shirley's*.'

25

Bertram sat at his office desk and stared at the letter which Joan had laid on his blotter. She did not wait while he read it, but hurried out, even she shorn, for once, of some of her poise by its contents.

Bertram read the letter twice, then twice again. It was unbelievable.

It was from the chairman of a group of department stores rooted in London, but with branches in several other towns, and stated that following recent negotiations with the principal shareholder the writer's company had acquired the controlling interest in the store. Because the name of Bliss was locally esteemed, it would be retained, and the board of directors hoped that Bertram too would stay in charge. An early meeting was proposed; till now, during the business transactions, secrecy had been essential lest rival firms entered the lists to bid for control.

As Bertram read, life went on, all unheeding, in the store around him. Along the corridor, typists worked, or giggled, or varnished their nails, as they had always done. In the cloakroom Hermione Tipps painted her eyelids emerald green and admired the minuscule diamond in her engagment ring. Down in the basement, Paul

Jessamy brooded among a consignment of Persian rugs and thought of writing to Harrods for a job. Young Joe whistled between his teeth as he arranged fireside chairs in echelon and dreamed of Hermione's soft, warm lips and plump, responsive body. The new assistant stacked lampshades tidily in sizes and longed for her coffee break. In Toiletries, Mildred Smith sprayed *Je Reviens* all round her neck and wondered if she would ever own a whole bottle. In Men's Wear, Mr. Thomas worried because his parrot's beak was dull and the bird was moulting freely. In Fashions, Maud Wilson, in charge while Eileen recovered from her attack of influenza, rearranged the dress racks in new places and planned a trip to the London wholesale houses in her senior's place.

Eileen was better, but still in bed. While Bertram sat in his office reading his letter, Shirley arrived to see her, early though it was. She came with a proposal so astounding that Eileen, in her weak state, could not at first understand what she was being told.

She looked amazed at Shirley as she repeated her remarks. Shirley was quite slim now, Eileen suddenly saw, and had lost the lethargy which once had characterised her. She seemed a little tense, but full of energy. It had taken her a very long time to rebel, but now the revolt was all the greater. Eileen soon agreed to leave the store and go into the boutique with Shirley. It was a good idea and would be successful, but what would Bertram say? Shirley did not seem to care.

Eileen saw that some profound metamorphosis had taken place, and thought back over the recent weeks. On Shirley's visit to London a short time ago she must have put in hand this business of her holding in the store; what a step to have taken, without consulting Bertram.

She decided not to ask questions to which she might never be told the answers. The boutique would be fun, and with their contacts it would thrive. It would not make much competition for Bliss's itself if they stocked mainly top-price goods, for which there was an increasing demand locally. Marjorie should be drawn into it too, Eileen resolved; they were sure to need a secretary as soon as they were established; it would be better for her than shadowing Joan for ever.

While Eileen pondered, and grew quite excited, Shirley drove home. She went up to her apricot bedroom and hung up her coat. Then she brushed her short hair; it was getting very grey : perhaps she would have some silver streaks put in to lighten it. She laid down her brush and turned away from the mirror to look at the apricot bed. It was going to be hers alone.

She moved all Bertram's possessions into his dressing-room. If he preferred, he could transfer to the larger spare bedroom; it was of no importance. All that mattered was that she should be alone. She had ordered new curtains, a new spread, and a new covering for the headboard, in primrose yellow; simple perhaps, but her own choice.

She went downstairs to the living-room. Bertram's desk was open, and his pile of stamp albums rested on it, left there the night before. She picked one up and turned the pages. She had thought of burning his collection. It was a crazy idea, she knew; perhaps she had been a little mad then, but she was quite sane now. Anyway, she had thought of a better idea.

Bertram was now the master of nothing.